THE MORE YOU IGNORE ME

THE MORE YOU IGNORE ME

A NOVEL

Travis Nichols

COFFEE HOUSE PRESS
MINNEAPOLIS
2013

COVER AND BOOK DESIGN by Linda Koutsky

Coffee House Press books are available to the trade through our primary distributor, Consortium Book Sales & Distribution, cbsd.com or (800) 283-3572. For personal orders, catalogs, or other information, write to: info@coffeehousepress.org.

Coffee House Press is a nonprofit literary publishing house. Support from private foundations, corporate giving programs, government programs, and generous individuals helps make the publication of our books possible. We gratefully acknowledge their support in detail in the back of this book.

Good books are brewing at coffeehousepress.org

LIBRARY OF CONGRESS CIP INFORMATION
Nichols, Travis, 1979–
The more you ignore me / Travis Nichols.
p. cm.
ISBN 978-1-56689-321-3 (pbk.)
I. Title.
PS3614.I3532M67 2013
813'.6—dc23
2012036526

FIRST EDITION / FIRST PRINTING
PRINTED IN THE UNITED STATES

ACKNOWLEDGMENTS
I would like to thank the wonderful staff of Coffee House Press for its support and encouragement, as well as Patrick Culliton, Stephen Danos, Katie Geha, Noah Eli Gordon, Emily Gould, Cathy Halley, Paul Killebrew, Dorothea Lasky, Dolly Lemke, Fred Sasaki, Justin Taylor, Brian West, Nicole Wilson, and Matthew Zapruder for their advice and astute analysis. Thanks to my family for everything inside as well as out, and I <3 Monica Fambrough forever for her insight, patience, and love.

THE MORE YOU IGNORE ME

Excellent point, cookiekitty7, one that most certainly deserves serious consideration, but before I address it I would like to bring another matter—of equal, or, perhaps, even, yes, *greater* (!!!) importance—to the group's attention.

First, though, let me say once again how happy I am to be here on this essential culinary site, where every recipe, opinion, viewpoint, and perspective is given the *consideration* it so richly deserves.

For this, I humbly thank you.

(THANK YOU!!!!!)

Tonight, friends, let us continue together in the grand tradition of online democratic society—rough, fragile experiment that it remains—in strict defiance of the forces dedicated to crushing it under the black boot heel of petty fascism.

Let us also say: welcome!

Welcome to all who have heretofore been shunted from society's fellowship because of their ability (and willingness!) to express unpopular but prescient opinions clearly, forcefully, and—this is crucial—without apology.

Welcome! Let us begin!

First, I admit I have hinted at this matter in previous comments (cf. "Yummy Vegetarian Lasagna for Two"), yet I have always hesitated bringing this case fully to bear for fear of what scandalous rumors and/or slanderous opinions might have previously crossed your screens.

But now I feel so strongly that for the good of our collective endeavor this issue *must* be brought up that I am disregarding the personal risk to my reputation such attention-bringing might afford, and I am plunging forward because this case has such grave repercussions for us all.

Risking everything on behalf of it is perhaps still not quite enough.

Now, normally, I am as light and carefree as the law allows, but for the past few months this matter has brought me terribly low.

Let me lay it plain: I have been, by a childish and ignorant member of the online community, banned.

More: My input regarding Charli and Nico's wedding is no longer even considered for publication!

I have no idea why, and no one will give me the courtesy of a proper response.

At first, I thought perhaps it was benign neglect, to re-appropriate a phrase, but I've since realized something much more sinister is afoot, so now—since I am no longer even *allowed* on Charlico.com—I am bringing this matter before you here on this august and humane recipe blog you call, surely in jest, BrendaCookingFun.com.

No doubt, scandalous rumors and libelous character assassinations have passed before your eyes, sent, as ever, by Charli and Nico's "best man," Chris Novtalis—that sulfurous toad, that young dullard, that tyrant erroneously allowed to be in charge of Charlico.com out of misguided goodwill or charity—but please hear me out.

I am just a citizen who wishes his voice not be silenced.

My banishment from Charlico.com has obviously been an immense personal loss for me, not only because I made so many wonderful friends and admirers through that site, but because together my *cortege* and I made great strides toward solving a number of problems of the world.

I know that sounds *grandiose,* but I firmly believe that, just as Margaret Mitchell once said, "A small number of devoted individuals can, in fact, change the course of history; Indeed, this is the only thing that ever has!"—yes, in my case, just look at the record!

Take heed!

It is all by some miracle still on the site for the world to see, if only said world could stop pursuing vile distraction long enough to read and take note.

It is shocking to see such truths laid out in plain sight, I know, but it is even more shocking to see them ignored, though I have come to expect no less from the sad excuse for "society" we float through.

Lest you get the wrong impression, let me be clear that I am not so narcissistic or naive as to think you would consider my personal loss, great as it is, worthy of your in-demand time. Not because you lack compassion! No, don't think I write tonight to insult you!

Fear not! Despite what you have heard of me, I am not that man.

No, you wouldn't consider my personal tragedy of much importance because you are spending your time working diligently to solve what you see as the great problems we all face in this fearful and horrid episode called "life."

Yes, but hear me out—my tragedy and the world's are not so different. No, in fact, shocking as it may sound, I believe they are ONE AND THE SAME!!!

The exclamation points, I know, seem out of place or perhaps too much, but you see I'm quite an exuberant fellow, a joyful soul, really, and I can let my emotions get the best of me like a schoolgirl face to face with a succulent lolly, but it is all only for the greater good since, as I hope you'll see, underneath the emotion there is cold hard reason, such that is missing greatly in this ill-begotten world of incorrigible ineptitude.

I have had so many—SO MANY!—friends and acquaintances tell me, at long last, that they see my point after all, and yes, it seems I was right all along, and had only exposed my solution with too bright a flash of rhetoric.

I am working on this admitted character flaw, but I hope you'll agree that it is a relatively minor one, especially when it is often the reader's own flaws that prevent him (or her!) from seeing my point.

A mere distraction, though. I'm quite likable, really.

In fact, I think we could be great friends if given the chance to meet, if I could be allowed to arrive at your very doorstep with a rose in my teeth (TRA LA!)

But let's not get too far ahead of ourselves.

You see, I would be perfectly willing to look past my own personal feelings of being slighted, abused, and wantonly rejected by this cruel and imagination-less "best man" if I weren't able to see in my personal issue the problems of the world.

I, a humble man of limited means, alone in life except for a vast but distant group of online peers, simply wanted to put my modest writerly talents to use in service of *gnosis*.

Contrary to what you might think, the fact that my banishment has become the central topic of discussion for this particular wedding and its affiliated blog does not in any way cloud my thinking about the overall concepts at play.

I see the "big picture" despite the bride's continued silence toward me (surely kept up on the advice of the groom's brother, the wretched best man and moderator, Chris Novtalis, who fancies himself some kind of chivalrous knight instead of, accurately, a bilious nuisance), and in fact, I did not even seek out that particular blog but rather had it thrust upon me by fate and simple geometry.

Triangles and pyramids, my dears!

Natural shapes, true, though they are not nearly as simple or as ordinary as they first appear, especially when they manifest themselves in human relationships, as they do more often than one might expect, if one knows *how* to look.

The impatient reader here surely asks, "Fascinating, but how does this revelation lead in any way to the full-blown catastrophe on the previously mentioned wedding blog?"

Gravioria manent, dear readers.

Gravioria manent.

Allow me a brief reminisce: I once had a particularly contentious encounter with a confused and dissolute young woman I like to call My First Love, or MFL.

We do not (yet!) need to go into detail about MFL, but suffice it to say that in the years since this encounter I have desperately wanted to explain myself more articulately to MFL, as well as to see what might have become of her, how she has developed both emotionally and physically in the time since our memorable encounter.

Despite these dreams—and despite my dedication—I have had little luck tracking MFL down in the "meat space," since it seems she refuses to register her utilities in her maiden name, nor will she list her phone number in the white pages of any conceivable locale.

Quite frustrating, yes, since I simply want to tell her that I misunderstood my role, lo those many years ago.

For reasons that seem silly now, it was, in the first few days of my unemployment, QUITE IMPORTANT for me to explain myself thusly to her, and my inability to find MFL began to cause me serious harm.

The dark folds began, once again, to smother and choke me.

But then—praise be!—fate intervened and my search for MFL became a mere prelude to this Charli matter.

Let me explain.

Since I had been given this gift of time away from employment, I embarked on a few long-delayed projects, including the aforementioned search for MFL, and one such project involved obtaining images of certain female politicians.

In the course of searching for a particularly choice candidate—one I will not name, for fear of giving her my unpaid endorsement—I came across a luminous image that was clearly A BOLT FROM BEYOND!

The image itself first appeared quite ordinary—"my" candidate waving smugly to a group of protesters—but in the background, in amongst this motley group, I spied a young brunette insouciantly waving a placard while staring directly into the camera's lens with a kind of *dégagé* pout that could not but stir a proper man's soul.

My eyes took in this young brunette—her gleaming doll's teeth, her eyes done up in slipshod shadow, her rabbit nostrils midquiver, all on display in the background of this idiotic campaign shot—and I immediately felt as if I had once again fallen through a wormhole into the past, for, dear readers, this young woman in the campaign photo looked EXACTLY like MFL as I had known her twenty years ago!

Are you still seated, readers?

Yes?

Then, I have not made myself clear.

How can I accurately explain the singularity of this?

It's not as if MFL had a common look—no, she seemed a one-of-a-kind beauty, a very particular taste, a young Ally Sheedy in a bulky sweater hiding quite an array of goodies—and so the idea that someone twenty years later would strike the same pose, cut the same profile, shock the same system . . . well, it might as well have been a narwhal leaping from a city sewer system to impale a passerby with its tusk.

What were the odds?

The odds were so improbable that the fact of this occurrence clearly indicated that the true structure of reality had been made manifest in our false world in order to tell me . . . what?

WHAT WAS THE TRUE STRUCTURE OF REALITY TRYING TO TELL ME?!?!?!

Perhaps, I thought then, slumped over my keyboard from mental fatigue, this young replica of MFL and I would have an opportunity to correct the mistakes of the past.

Perhaps, I thought, brightening, there may indeed be second acts in life.

Perhaps, yes, I sat up straight, I do have one or two adventures left in this dim interval.

Perhaps there is a reason I have been cast aside from the workaday world.

Perhaps I do indeed have a purpose in this new millennium!

I lifted my head from atop my keyboard, raised my fist to the sky, and yelled, "YES!!!!"

I made a personal vow then and there to investigate, for, if given the chance, I would do everything in my power to give this new young woman the benefit of my love!!!!!

Unbowed by the tracking devices surely installed in the search engine I am forced to use, I set to work with my detective skills and unsurpassed vigor to uncover the identity of this young beauty.

In no time—never mind how, ye cops!—I had a name: Charli Vistons.

And—in a blink—I had a Facebook page.

Wondrous bounty!

I deliriously noted her interests and affiliations, her likes and (implied) dislikes, all laid bare for the world to see like some streetwalker's tawdry wares, and, dear readers, disappointment did not touch me, for Charli was not only the very image of MFL, but it seemed she possessed the spirit of MFL as well!

Salinger, the Beatles, Dusty Springfield, *Harold and Maude*, the *Umbrellas of Cherbourg*—it was all the same!

I felt the stars aligning after noting that Charli lived a mere hundred miles from me, a day's journey, and she worked semipublicly "on campus" as a "Film Studies Teaching Associate" at *my very alma mater.*

Film studies!

It truly was all happening again!

I began an itinerary in my head, had gotten halfway down the interstate of my mind, in fact, when I saw—brutal fate!—that Charli was "in a relationship."

Dagger!

What was this twist?

Worse, it seemed she was to be—ah—married.

And soon!

Samsara had seen fit to deal me yet another blow, eh?

I shook my fist at the ceiling, then out the window at the sky.

I rent my night garment (still worn from the previous night) and clawed at my chest.

After a few long minutes of this, I found I could not ignore my feelings any longer, and so in a flurry of clicks and scrolls I delved further into the life of Charli Vistons, obstacles be damned!

I saw, of course, that the young beauty's fiancé was a rotund pud of a man named Nico, unworthy of her succulent charms.

I admit, this was more than a bit shocking—surely she could do better?—but I followed the chain duly, hoping to find some indication that Charli would not be throwing her life away, that perhaps her fiancé was handsome *on the inside.*

Sadly, he was just as dull and insipid, it seemed, inside as he was out.

Thinking Nico's Facebook profile might offer a different and perhaps better perspective on Charli's situation, I clicked on each morsel offered there until I arrived, finally, on a link to the dire and garish wedding website, Charlico.com.

I stayed there, despite the insult to my sensibility, in good faith.

Once there on the "splash page," I felt I had sufficiently calmed down—I admit I can get carried away—and could accept whatever role in Charli's life destiny assigned me: teacher, lover, admirer, friend.

I knew I could still help Charli—which, dear readers, is all I have ever wanted to do!—but I knew even then I must be judicious about my battles. I couldn't simply heave myself headlong into her life.

That was, of course, the mistake I had made with MFL.

So, how to approach Charli?

Would her "wedding" really happen?

Was the whole thing as ghoulish as it seemed?

The hidden world does reveal itself to us, readers, if only we take the time to look.

I proceeded with my clicking, and, thinking I was headed to Charlico.com's "registry," where I could perhaps offer some consumer advocacy, I must have misclicked in a moment of inattention, for lo, I found myself unwittingly "on the blog."

My browsing history reveals that this fatal act happened in the small hours of a Wednesday morning.

Immediately upon load of the Charlico.com/blog page, I became confused.

Society had clearly declared to me on numerous occasions that weddings were private celebrations restricted from public online discussion, and yet, here was a wedding website with a very public blog?!?!

Why?

Momentarily perplexed, the thought came suddenly that perhaps this wedding party wanted to discuss *the issues*!

Yes, of course!

That is why lovely Charli had a wedding blog!

For me!

Maybe there was hope after all, maybe, I said to myself. I could not only scrub my past clean, but also strike out anew with a joyous community!

Naively renewed, I dedicated myself to studying the behavior on the blog, cataloging the speakers, the arguments, and the ever-present rhetorical follies. It was a time of study.

The facts: Here were two young people without real jobs, prospects, or ideology, set to marry in the countryside out of, one assumes, boredom—an everyday occurrence, nothing special, and yet, I felt, in this case, it was somehow indeed extraordinary.

At first I couldn't quite put my finger on why.

True, the principal players resembled some from my past, but I vowed not to let the Personal distract me from the larger issues at hand, for beyond the resemblances to my previous intimate entanglement (MFL), and despite the poor match between Charli and Nico, I felt there was the potential for something special here.

But what?

I continued my observations, and despite what you might think (and, I admit, despite what I initially predicted), I found the perspectives of the young people on the blog to actually be quite engaging.

In fact, after a time, I found them peculiarly resplendent with compassion, wit, and intellectual vigor.

Believe me, I was as surprised as you.

The more I read, the more I found in these voices a rare potential to bring into being a true haven, a shelter from the worldly storm of sorrow and strife, a space where a small group of forward thinkers could discuss *the issues* without society's censors concealing them.

I had found kindred spirits dedicated to the free exchange of ideas, and I thought I could content myself by simply observing and taking note.

Soon though, it became clear the blog was missing a key element, a sagacity that comes with age that could activate the yeast, as it were, and bring the loaf of true thought into the world. The blog was missing my presence.

So, gingerly at first, I tried out my own voice in a meek little comment on a now-forgotten post (cf. "Alternate directions to the Clark House Inn"), and, gracious, I found that I was embraced!

Cousin_Kevin said, and I quote from memory, "It's true that there is quite the 'wedding industry,' but I don't think we REALLY need to go on and on about it here, dude. Congrats, Charlico!"

When I read this response to my meager posting, I'm not ashamed to say it was one of the happiest days of my life.

Truly!

And so many wonderful days ensued of adroit badinage (I won't deny that I took great pleasure in the back and forth) that I literally lost track of time, spending hours upon hours engaged in joyous debate with all comers—Linksys181, Cousin_Kevin, NICO!, Emma_1, and, yes, even Chris.

Dear readers, it was then that I understood this blog itself offered the revolution I had been searching for. Why? Because this seemingly private blog offered FREE AND OPEN COMMENTS!

The personal is absolutely political, after all.

Of course blog comments in general, dear readers, are revolutionary because they allow for point X, which dilates our triangular perception from simple A, B, and C into the pyramidal realms.

Before comments, we all thought only in these paltry terms: "words = writer/reality."

Now, of course, it seems comical to those of us *in the know* that anyone would live such a restricted life, but, dear readers, many still do to this day!

The words these ignorant saps read, the worlds they assume, are only bound manifestations of various writers' consciousnesses mingling with reality, and so unwittingly these "readers" literally TAKE THE WRITERS' WORDS FOR IT—"it" in this case being the very reality we drift through on a daily basis.

!!!!!!!!

As we know, comments change all of this.

On a blog with comments, the writer and his reality mingle to make the words as ever—but outside, on a separate plane, the commenter is THERE evaluating this mingling manifestation, weighing veracity and fidelity on the scales of justice.

And he will not keep quiet!

No, the true commenter alone advocates on behalf of reality unbeholden, and so now, with comments, we have a new equation:

$$\frac{\text{Words = Writer/Reality}}{\text{COMMENTER}}$$

And thus a new, expanded universe!

The true commenter takes nothing at face value but remains intractably, joyously skeptical of any purported reality.

Of course, most commenters don't take advantage of this coveted position.

Most commenters simply parrot the writer's version of reality with hopes of some condescending pat on the head—sad!—but the form itself is revolutionary, for even in the seeming non sequitor spam comment soliciting consumers for penile enhancement, our conception of reality has been, yes, enhanced!

And so, in this spirit, on Charlico.com/blog, I saw suddenly how I would be able to enhance this wedding party's reality.

If allowed to reach its full potential, the blog and its commenters could be, I thought, yes, a harbinger of beautiful things to come, for I saw quite clearly that the wedding blog's comments *existed* for me, in order to facilitate my role within Charli's life.

The comments were a gift from the *gnosis,* delivered so I could have the opportunity to not only be of use to the young, but to cleanse my soul of clinging problems of the past.

Thus, with hopes high, still unaware of the pyramid's exact dimension or how exactly I would perform, once again, the role of point X, I began my initiative.

Happy?

Yes.

But even in those delirious hours, despite my happiness, I sensed a lurking evil.

Something was not quite right.

It was as if, hidden beneath the floorboards of our meticulously constructed yet still tenuous shelter, the carcass of some dead mammal sat decomposing in a riot of flies, maggots, and brainy juice, out of sight of casual onlookers, threatening to undermine with its rot whatever foundation might have been established above.

How could I tell something was wrong?

Easy.

After every true comment I made, a snide, mocking tone emerged from the false commenters in response, first from just one, then from another, and then commenter after commenter began chortling at my (correction: *our*) earnest striving toward a better tomorrow, as if I/we were a kind of amusing mascot rather than a sage.

Being a sensitive sort, as well as a seasoned hand at online discussion, I did not simply "let it go," as I have often been advised to do.

Oh, yes, how many times have I been told to ignore my feelings, bottle them up, and simply skip on down the path to another web community.

I can even hear you now—"*Web* community? What about life away from the computer? A family? A garden? Go for a walk! Ride a bike! Get away from the screen!"

You can never know it, but how cruel such remarks are to me.

You see, I cannot.

There are reasons, even those besides the fact that when I do journey to different web communities I feel—no, I know!—that the impetuous twerp Chris Novtalis is on Charlico.com/blog working away to undo all of my efforts.

He's fanning the flames of rumor, innuendo, and, yes, a legal term is necessary: defamation.

He wouldn't have an online community—a reason to live?—if it weren't for me, but he goes on day after day taunting me.

He deploys the letters of my name in muddled anagrammical jibes at my character, he reworks my carefully wrought language in pathetic efforts to take credit for my ideas, and then, of course, he makes direct attacks on my good name and character.

Chris, this peasant of a man, telling his vast and undeserved audience that I am "psychotic" and "boring" and "not even a part of the wedding."

Boring!

Is that a capital offense now?

God forbid I would bore such a fertile mind as that bloodsucker has!

Boring!

From such a racist, sexist, classist, ageist Neanderthal I suppose I should see that as a compliment!

But, alas, I cannot.

I see it for what it is: a base and degrading insult from an inferior.

Do you want to know what happens when I try to "move on," as you suggest?

Do you?

Well, I'll tell you.

I get heart palpitations.

I get night sweats.

I'm sure I run a fever (though I haven't confirmed due to a childhood trauma involving thermometers).

A heavy, static-filled succubus sits on my neck, jams its arm down my throat, and stops up my breath until I force myself to go to the computer to see what vile filth is cascading down the corridors of the internet unchecked while I've been away.

And every time, I find that I am right! There it is! It is ALWAYS there—and worse than I imagined!

Hear me out: Like everyone else, I wake up each morning. A deceptively simple phrase, true, but what a gift! I am grateful!

This morning, for example, in the dank June air, consciousness broke over me like a pane of glass, and for a few minutes I felt free and clear of strife, anxiety, and horror.

I thought I might take in a film or eat a nice apple, work on a screen or teleplay. In short, live my life. But then, I remembered.

I thought of the putrid excrescence spewing out into the world as I was lying there, and so I lurched from my cot to my desk and I turned on the computer.

Horror! Filth!

I admit, because he is a crafty little devil, sometimes I think of the runty, Skittle-brained moderator and chuckle, *Oh, that's all he's got?*

Sometimes I even leave the room, go buy my meager rations (as my submitted recipes indicate, I cook everything in my coffeemaker—instantly!—oatmeal, polenta, Tasty Bite Indian cuisine, rice; it's an ingenious system, if I may pay myself that compliment, and quite cost-effective considering my "condition"), but while I'm out a phrase or even the subtle implication of a phrase inevitably comes crashing back into my mind, where it festers and oozes until I'm back at my "desk," blinded by fury.

I'm surprised I can even type. But type I must! And what does he want? Finally, what does this goon want?

Only the complete annihilation of my person, my history, and, I suppose, my ideas.

I believe he would kill me, given the chance, and so I am justified in my actions because it is a fight to the death. It is truly either him or me, and I am not one to back down!

Why does he hate me so?

Because I know that he has plans for the bride.

Shocking?

Yes.

Quite.

But you should know that I don't level this accusation lightly or without merit. I know, because I did not let it go. No, I began to investigate further.

As many of you know, I soon pulled back the floorboard in question and uncovered the stinkmaker, the sock-puppet handler, the chortler, the fascist, the overweening point C of the love triangle:

Chris Novtalis!!!!

Assassin!

Yes, I was as shocked as anyone that it turned out to be the BEST MAN and WEDDING BLOG MODERATOR, who, I might as well make it plain again here, had (and has!) plans not only to degrade the *idea* of marriage, but to ravish the bride, Charli, and destroy her happiness with lusty violation *in flagrant delicto*!

Those who do not study history, etc.

I know at first you will doubtlessly find it at best *curious* that someone with coital plans for the bride would be such a vocal cheerleader for a marriage involving, primarily, his brother, but don't let the blinders society has saddled you with restrict your reason.

Remember the basics of geometry, my dears, for Chris surely does.

He wishes to assume the role of C, to shoot his line straight through Charli's B, obliterating Nico's A.

Squirp is the horrendous noise I imagine this act making.

Squirp.

Squirp.

Squirp.

Over and over again!

For you see, Chris does not wish to expand the triangle into a pyramid, but rather to reduce it to a fascist line.

Clearly, Chris wants this marriage to go forward simply so he can have dear Charli close at hand, as part of his "family," and thus within his filthy reach in order to violate her repeatedly and at will behind the back of his sad, pathetic brother Nico (point A).

This would, of course, simply be hurtful toward Nico and destructive to Charli (i.e., none of my business), if it weren't symptomatic of the larger issues at play.

Proof?

My word is not good enough for you?

Well, I can't blame you, since most of you aren't aware of my record as online justice-seeker and truth-teller, so how about this, an e-mail I received from "Charli" soon after my campaign began. I present it here in toto:

Hello,

I don't know who you are, or why you write the terrible things that you do on our website, but I'm writing today to ask you to please stop.

Please do not comment anymore on our blog. It is hurtful and destructive. Please. Just stop.

You're a writer, a real one, and I respect your gifts. As you know, I'm a writer too, and so I know what it's like to be misunderstood.

I'm guessing from what you've written in the comments that you feel like you aren't in control of the narrative of your life. People—on our blog, and I'm sure elsewhere—accuse you of being a number of things you swear you are not. I believe you.

But I have to tell you: your writing only makes it worse.

This is hard to understand, I know, because it's clear that all you have ever done is write in an attempt to give shape to what you've called "the lurching chaos of our time." You say you've begun to feel like "an emptied-out version of what you had hoped you'd be," and I don't doubt it. But this is not the answer.

I'm sure you don't believe me when I say I understand, but maybe I can prove it to you.

Years ago Nico read hurtful things I had once written about him in my journal. I was trying to weigh the pros and cons of staying with him after a fight, and I wrote down thoughts I would never say aloud in an attempt to understand my own muddled thinking. Nico read these thoughts—never mind how—and our relationship nearly didn't recover. In fact, to this day I've felt only dread and paranoia when I've written anything down—even this e-mail—worried I'll somehow hurt him again without intending to.

To make matters worse, for some reason Nico showed his mother what I had written. This woman is soon to be my mother-in-law. When she finished reading she said, jokingly, to Nico: "I'm not sure I should've let you shack up with that bitch!"

You see, I was misunderstood. Just like you.

Or how about this:

A film studies student of mine who was upset about his grade put e-mails I wrote to him up on his blog—along with pictures of me taken from my friends' public Flickr accounts, some of them in my bathing suit. Other former students of mine, all male, wrote terrible, hurtful things about me in the comments, but what could I do? Write in and tell them to stop looking? Of course not. Sometimes, you have to just let it go.

I'm begging you, as a sympathetic friend, to please do just that. Whatever has caused you to latch on to us, please, just let it go. Please, please leave us alone.

Sincerely,
Charli

Well, dear readers, I must tell you this ruse nearly worked. I felt touched in my very soul by these hysterical words, ashamed that I had caused Charli to feel further misery when all I had wanted was to love her. So much strife! She sounded deranged!

Had I caused her so much trouble merely by *commenting*?

My god!

But then I thought, Isn't it CONVENIENT for her to have had so many similar experiences at her fingertips, ready to be deployed at just the right moment? Isn't the language employed to convey these feelings a bit TOO deranged and yet still precise? Isn't this e-mail a bit too, dare I say, mannered?

Yes, of course it was!

Because it wasn't Charli at all!

It was Chris *himself* who must have sent this epistle from Charli's account!!!!!

It was the only explanation, since I know she couldn't truly want me to stop enlightening her.

Nice try, scoundrel!

I copied the false letter in its entirety and posted it on the blog for the community to see, and just like clockwork I received the following note from Chris, the Charlico.com/blog "moderator," whom I'm sure must have been appointed to his position on a day in which the bride was too overtaxed to see he is, in fact, retarded.

Now, don't take offense—I don't use the word "retarded" to put down the disabled but rather to illustrate in the most succinct way possible that this horrid cur is *malformed*, that something must have gone wrong very early, in the womb perhaps, or even in the very first coupling of DNA strands; a fateful deficiency of protein or glucose caused him to take on that slack-jawed look, that high slope of forehead, and that squeezed-melon of a skull.

How sad his mother must have been when she beheld him in the nursery!

I don't doubt she considered heaving such a creature into a dumpster on her way home, or smothering him with her begowned belly whilst still in her hospital bed.

And if she had!

How we would have been so happily spared such trouble! ☺:

Hey ***hole,

**** you, you ****ing piece of diseased intestinal waste.

Fun time is over.

If you publish one more comment, send one more e-mail, leave one more voicemail, contact me, Nico, Charli, or anyone else in the family in any way again, I will ****ing kill you.

You are a sociopath.

Seek help.

If I see you on the street—ever—I will push your ****ing teeth in with the heel of my hand.

I will rip your nostrils out with my fingers and shove the little flaps of skin down your throat until you choke.

I will cut you from your ****** to your scalp with my **** and **** in your chest cavity, you *******.

**** you.

**** off.

Die.

—Chris

Oh my!

I am aghast even to cut and paste such filth into this post.

I vow to, as far as I am able, keep my comments free from the language implied by the asterisks, but you see I must give you a sense of what I'm up against.

You need to be shown the truth so you can see how troubled your own online endeavors—your *life's work*—might be at this very moment!

For if any of you are sheltering or employing a wretch like Chris, let's be clear: you are abetting criminal activities that will not go unpunished.

I mean, my nostrils!?

I believe, dear me, he would, too!

How was this person given any authority at all?

The mind reels.

I know I should go to the police with such a threat, and no doubt that is what you will advise me to do—or may even be doing yourself at this very moment—but please, hear me out.

The police?

I do not want the police.

Not yet.

It is possible to solve this without getting the State involved, though I am, of course, keeping all the correspondence from this sorrowful episode on file, just in case.

I have found records such as these useful in the past.

In fact, it is thanks to my record keeping that I was exonerated, officially cleared of any wrongdoing, in that infamous case years ago with MFL, which I may have occasion to revisit with you at some point in the future.

Rest assured that those points A and B got their comeuppance—and more!—once I was released from the hospital (C got his, of course, but I was not at fault).

In fact, there are a few choice details from that affair no one has yet turned up, and if the time is ever right and you turn out to be the compassionate and trustworthy compatriots (or compatriotesses!) I assume you to be, then I daresay I will let you in on it.

My word!

I've gone off again!

I must be subconsciously trying to distance myself from those hateful and poisonous attacks sent to me before and quoted above (defecate in my chest cavity? That does NOT sound sanitary ☺).

But—Chris's words—there they are.

As frightful as they may be for you to look at, think of me!

I have to live with them!

A man is never a prophet in his own country.

I believe this is the saying.

But what of a man with no country?

Might he be recognized as a prophet simply because he has no local pharmacist, no chauffeur, no passel of gossiping ladies to destroy his reputation from inside out?

Sadly, in my case, it seems I am not to be recognized as a prophet anywhere but scorned forever everywhere, even after my detractors see the light and come to accept—embrace, even!—my ideas.

All continue to shun me as if no one had thrown the cold water of reality and reason on their fevered brains.

But not just reality and reason, passion and wit too!

The future!

As seems to be the case with my own (now estranged) family.

But what—in the parlance of the woeful "millennial" generation—are my "probs" with this marriage?

What does the world so desperately need to hear that I would take the risk tonight (and every night!) to defend my ideas so brazenly?

Why do I continue to offer my admittedly unsolicited advice and prognostications if I am, as they've stated so clearly, not a "part of the wedding?"

These questions sadden me, dear readers.

I have answered them repeatedly on Charlico.com/blog, but I understand many of you are occupied day and night with your own crusades, so you may not have followed my links and/or seen every subsequent argument to its conclusion, or, at the very least, given each thread the careful attention it deserves.

But fear not!

I have saved each exchange (with annotations and further commentary when necessary), and so I can offer you this peek into the veritable buffet of insight I have offered up to these callous nincompoops.

The following Charlico.com/blog comments come from late April, when the last snow had melted away and the first robin had begun its ruddy chirrup:

April 27, 2009 5:45PM
Emma_1: The menu looks AMAZING you guys!!! Make sure you take time out to ENJOY the DAY!!!!

April 27, 2009 6:07PM
linksys181: There will be no enjoyment.
Meals for this couple will be an ordeal.

April 27, 2009 6:21PM
Emma_1: Ha!
Funny!
Seriously tho I'm SO happy for NICO & CHARLI!!!! XOXOXO

April 27, 2009 6:22PM
linksys181: Serious?
Quite.
Why will their meals be ordeals? Fact: When one becomes married, each and every desire becomes a subject for discussion.
Has this occurred to you, Emma_1?
No, surely it has not, or you would respond with a mite more intelligence. Thought: Is one hungry?
Is one *married* and hungry?
Yes? Then one knows that before one can answer even such a basic question of hunger or satiety one must consider whether or not it is the proper time for one's "partner" to eat, too. But what if one's "partner" is already eating with another "partner"?
Do you see? *Eating*?
Partners?
Hmmm?

Must I make it even plainer for you?
The body is a complicated site of negotiation, and, I fear, at most, it takes two to tango.
Three's a crowd. Four's the semaphore.

April 27, 2009 6:27PM
Emma_1: LOL!!!

April 27, 2009 6:30PM
linksys181: LOL?
LOL?!?
Oh no, my dear.
Not LOL.
Not at all. Do not betray your gender with these trifling giggles.
Consider this: Is one sleepy?
Would sleep be required at this time?
Once again, a simple question UNLESS ONE IS ALSO UNWITTINGLY ENTERING INTO A MÉNAGE À TROIS!
In that case, one may not be able to sleep if one's "partner" is, for example, humping along on top of your delicate body, spilling drool into your tear-filled eyes behind your true "partner"'s back!

April 27, 2009 6:31PM
linksys157: I concur!
Marvelous point!

April 27, 2009 6:32PM
linksys181: Thank you, friend, whoever you are. (The troops are rallying!)
But let's not place the blame entirely on the husband for being such an ineffectual ninny.
Think of his (heh) position: Would one like an unbearable desire quenched quickly?
Well, one must wait until one's "partner" also desires to be

quenched, or one must act in a manner unbecoming a gentleman, or one must throw off the entire cycle of hunger and satiety by quenching one's desire oneself with whatever means one has at hand.

April 27, 2009 6:34PM
linksys157: So true!
And if one happens to be "caught" in the act of "personal" quenching? Repeatedly? With whatever is "at hand" (here, we can admit an LOL, can we not?
YES! LOL!).
Well, that personal quenching will be seen as neglecting the communal essence pot (or some such nonsense), and so one will thus be cast out of one's marriage bed.
And for what?
For lack of understanding on the part of the wife regarding what a self-obliterating undertaking marriage is for the husband. And for lack of understanding on the part of the husband that a "wife" is not for bedding in certain manners at all hours, even if she is not, as the case may be, carrying on with the "groom's closest relation" (Have we said too much?).One will emerge unrecognizable from such a marriage, if one emerges at all.

April 27, 2009 6:37PM
linksys181: We are truly coming to a consensus here.
I thank you, friend!
But why this pernicious silence from the rest of the Charlico community? Are the community members vexed as to why we reveal these facts to you rather than blithely applaud the *menu* and the *flower arrangements*? Simple: I believe Nico (and any other such bridegrooms) should know the truth of their potential "partnerships" if we are ever to have a truly egalitarian society (Yes, community, I am advocating for societal revolution. Does that scare you?

What of your precious "Obama," your "Xbox"? You will not need, dears, Obamas or Xboxes in my society. Why?

What will you do with your time?

I will answer a question with a question: What is the first requirement of a revolutionary, according to Che Guevara?

No, not an Xbox.

It is love, my dears!

Love! And what kind of love?

Love of truth, surely! And don't we all believe we have within ourselves a capacity for love?

I know I have love to give! Who will dare to take it?

You?

Take the challenge, community! TAKE IT!)

April 27, 2009 6:37PM

linksys157: I will take it, friend!

I accept your love of truth, and I will match it with my own truth-love in time (How I love this blog! What a wonderful space in which we can truly, honestly DISCUSS!). What we have revealed is, of course, just one set of facts that should be known by a man (or woman!) when entering into a union. There are more sets. And so you see we are merely providing a service.

When my revolutionary compatriots and I find a couple clearly unprepared for such tasks (Nico and Charli, in this case), we endeavor to be cruel, yes, but cruel to be kind with our "comments." Have we grown so sensitive that we can't stand the truth delivered with such style?

Surely not! Truth and beauty, my dear!

Let's not forget them. I await your response.

April 28, 2009 2:01AM

linksys181: I see by your continued silence, dear Emma_1, that we have perhaps gone too far in this initial conversionary tactic and stunned you into (further) dumbness.

I apologize if my remarks offend your delicate sensibility, but, alas, the truth is not delicate!
I was not spared.
DO NOT LOOK AWAY!!!!
FACE THE TRUTH!!!!!!

Readers, a blog "encourages" discussion, does it not?

Without comments, a weblog is merely a monologue, correct?

And I have, as you can see, discussed.

I have commented.

I have put forth my views, my warnings, my style, my beliefs, my visions of the future, and despite the efforts of this wretched Chris Novtalis to block me, I believe we have had a discussion.

Would it surprise you to know that after the exchange quoted above I received my first "warning" from Chris, the head of his private online neo-Stasi?

It's true, and I admit I was less than surprised since I had revealed quite a bit of his plot to the community.

Oh, it hasn't always been "me" putting forth my views (linksys181 and linksys157 are just two of the many masks I wear).

In fact, no one had discovered my "real" name for quite some time, and I am of course clever enough to cover my "cyber tracks," so I assumed I could not be traced.

I was able to persist through the resistance and mockery ("Are you really trolling a wedding website?" "STOP THE MADNESS," and so forth) until I was tarnished (again!) and dismissed (again!).

Treachery!

It pains me terribly.

Which is why I am now reaching out to you, dear readers, for I have been blocked, banned, and cast aside like some 19th-century madwoman. ☹

But what concern could any of this possibly be of yours?

I am sorry—a man can go on all night when he is in front of the computer screen.

What a cold light it gives off!

Not flattering to my features in the least, though I dare say I look a robust and vigorous forty-two.

I keep my goatee trim and wash my face with a secret astringent tincture every morning (in due time, my dears, in due time, I may tell you its components), so that even in the silver light of the screen I do not look such a cold fish.

I may, depending on how this goes, even attach a self-portrait for you.

Would you like that?

I daresay you might!

Here!

I am embedding it!

Keep it close to you, saucies!

[xxxxxxx]

I have been shunned.

That is what I mean to say.

I wish I could say I'm not used to such treatment, but I have been rejected, ignored, flung aside, and left for dead many times in life.

Oh, you have no idea!

From the very start!

You see, my own father was a navy man, and he had the terrible misfortune to sire me only months before shipping off with the USS *Maddox*.

Does that name ring a bell?

Or are you also of this idiotic generation that only knows the names of Ke$ha's entourage and not of those woefully mistreated, abused, and perhaps even murdered in the name of freedom for the United States of America?

I love this country.

I do.

I love it with all my heart, but I fear it has gone terribly astray.

It showed a small flicker of hope in the last century, but that hope has been snuffed out, that love has been squandered, and not as it was in my dear father's time, for something we all could believe in, but for baubles and trinkets!

The Indians have their revenge, eh?

We bought this land from them for costume jewelry, and we'll give the soiled remains back because we're so distracted by, what, celebrity "panties"?

Yes.

What a cruel and incomprehensible world this is!

And my case, what I'm presenting to you, is but a meager manifestation of this cruelty and incomprehensibility.

But for that very reason—because it is a miniscule capitulation to idiocy—we must not yield!

Don't look away!

Join me in reclaiming the righteous path!

It is not too late, despite what pernicious logorrhea you may have been subjected to by that ungrateful, small-minded, dime-store Hitler of a moderator Charli has in her employ.

Oh what a fateful day it was when she accepted that scallywag and allowed him to "moderate" her site!

I'm sure he arrived stinking of cologne, glad-handing and flattering the "wedding party," lulling them into thinking he might, with his modest credentials, youthful zeal, and relation to the groom, help steer their site safely through the perilous waters into a snug harbor.

What a light touch on the wheel that would have required!

The conversations, the ideas, the *esprit de corps* all arrived with me and began thriving, but then he strolled in with his wretched usurping arrogance to ask, "What is your problem?"

All he had to do was make sure someone kept the power on, since I was not just without problem, I had turned his wedding blog into a study in vitality!

On the precipice of real change!

But then the sulphurous bean decided to make everyone "register as family."

Oh ho!

Isn't that always the first step?

But register we did, "family" or no!

At first, I merely wanted to continue my observation of the wedding's progression, but soon I saw there was no one else brave enough to warn the couple of the dangers lurking in their false marriage bond.

It had to be me, though not because I disapproved of the marriage as such. No, don't take me for one of those men who think no one is good enough for "their" girls.

Those pathetic dolts are laughable. I live in the real world. I am aware. But you see, I am a feminist.

Does it shock you?

From all you've heard, I wouldn't doubt if it did shock you terribly, but it's true!

Of course I am not a feminist in the shrieking harpy sense of the word—I don't burn unmentionables on the post office steps or advocate for conspicuous armpit hair or free tampon dispensers at state parks—rather, I believe women should have the option to refuse the persistent, throbbing needs of men.

Without society judging them ill, women should be able to take up a life free of penetration, a life of chaste contemplation perhaps, of study, or of devotion to service.

The mothering instinct should not be wrung dry and made to sag by birth—don't we already have a population problem?—but allowed to fit snugly into the care of orphans, the elderly, and perhaps aged family members in need of professional and domestic assistance.

Marriage is an unhappy tradition in even the best circumstances, and it need not be unduly perpetuated, especially when it is merely a screen for a dark force to satisfy its oily urge!

This is my credo, and I would (and have!) fought for it outside of my own personal interest.

I know from experience. Am I wrong? Is the divorce rate in this country not astronomical? Statistics would be my second in this duel, if I needed a second.

I do not.

I admit, I am now personally invested in this case, but I hope you see that my *personality* isn't all I have invested.

If I were only to see the personal, I would say that obviously someone needs to care for Charli, fragile thing that she is, and perhaps Nico, the hulking sad sack, is the best she thinks she can do.

That's fine.

But if I could speak to her directly I would say, Sweet child, don't go into this lifelong union *unaware*!

That is all I ask!

Don't unwittingly enter into some disgusting *ménage a trois* with rival brothers without having your consent solicited!

Good God, isn't it obvious what is going on?

I see it all so clearly and remain stunned that I am the only one.

Since Chris had clearly forced Charli to ignore my repeated direct queries to her, I intended to accept my banishment once I imparted to Nico the necessary information about what his brother was up to.

But now, after the blog has been derailed so completely by nattering silliness after my banishment, it has become plain that Nico cannot rightly see his best man's plan to snuff out all purity and light from this world, and so I must take up the cudgel where I can.

Fellow commenters, hear me: this best man is a *beast* man!

I refuse to "let it go."

Why?

Because as soon as I began my revelatory task on Charlico.com/blog, Chris began his efforts to silence me, and such fascist oppression is the first step toward societal breakdown.

Scale does not matter.

Some details: Chris no longer just "warned" me; instead he began to "moderate" my comments, and soon thereafter to delete them before they were ever made public.

Of course!

He couldn't believe someone had uncovered his plot, and so he panicked in the grand tradition of the despot.

Oh, despite what you might think, I'm not writing to enlist you in my cause, as such. No! I wouldn't expect you to be so easily won over, though if even just one of you were to see reason, how close you would be, how *useful* to such a cause you could be!

Listen!

Some otherwise benign afternoon while that vile reed sits in his "moderator" chair, leaning back with a self-satisfied smirk on his face after typing in some banality, you could lean over him—so close that your auburn hair gently touches his temples, and your sparkling green eyes meet his only a few inches away.

He'd smell your shampoo, Garnier Fructis, and his little smirk would turn into something else entirely, a smile of genuine joy at your presence—he might even think of his mother, how she cared for him despite his obvious illegitimate monstrosity, and then you could stab him in the larynx repeatedly with a Rollerball Number 2 pen.

No one would blame you!

Blood would gush over his pathetic skinny tie, his Banana Republic shirt, and his seedy sport coat. He'd start grabbing at his throat, but unable to stop the spurting blood, wide-eyed, mouthing "help," he'd turn abruptly and fall, bloody neck pulp first, onto his keyboard and expire.

And there you would be, exhilarated, pen in hand, the heroine!

Your peers would, I'm sure, applaud you!

But of course this is a mere fantasy, a joke even!

Not a threat!

I am aware none of this site's readers share an office with Chris.

Surely he is just a hired hand, a "freelancer" who "telecommutes" to Charlico.com/blog.

But some of you *do* have contact with him.

I know that to be true from my observations here.

You are not innocent in this crime, though I allow you are "not guilty" in the sense that up until now you perhaps were unaware of all that plagued you.

But let's not dwell on that fact.

I obviously don't need violence to defeat this grunting fetus.

I have my nimble wit and the power of the truth at my fingertips!

He cannot hide from the truth, which is that he has once again attempted to silence the wrong man!

I will not go quietly nor gently!

I will rage!

I will not roll over and let his filthy fingers worm their way into my rectum in an obscene bid to give sick pleasure.

It's only he who enjoys such vices—not I!

And surely not you, my sweet ones!

You wouldn't (and surely haven't!) knowingly rolled over for him, though I know young women in our horrid cities feel the need to do awful things to validate themselves from time to time because of our diseased culture.

A girl doesn't seem to feel any sense of self-worth unless some man is making a film of her with a miniature baseball bat crammed halfway up her vaginal cavity.

It's awful.

She might even give it a little flex so the knob of the bat wiggles in the putrid air of her bedroom and think such a thing is somehow appealing, or that it is a point of pride to be able to do such a thing with a vulgar pornographer.

But my dears, any reasonable man will just feel contempt for you.

Trust me.

No man wants to follow a baseball bat.

Even a miniature one!

Though I daresay it might be preferable to following that sewer of a moderator.

But what am I saying!?

I would forgive you!

A drunken night can lead a girl to think it necessary to allow the fingers of a man to enter her as she lies nearly passed out . . . you're impressionable, I know, but I promise I won't take advantage that way.

Hear me out.

I merely want justice served.

The wedding plans proceed, and the procession grates against my sensibility, but action is still possible!

I know Chris feels my presence.

I nag at his conscience.

How do I know?

Because I analyze data.

I know where to get information.

I will soon have a site of my own, and then I will see when he checks up on me, on what I've been saying and doing.

He will soon be watching *my* every move!

He won't miss a day!

He won't be able to help himself.

Perhaps he's even here now, having followed me to this very recipe site tonight.

Hello!

Smile for the birdie!

I *dare* you to do something!

The comments are open, are they not?

Scum!

What's that?

Nothing?

No response?

You cheap tyrants are all the same.

You can't stand any voice of reason intruding on your fantasies of power and domination.

Say something, Ayatollah!

I dare you!

Come into this world and see how it feels to be treated as I've been treated by you, like an invisible!

I exist!

I will prove it to you!

Oh you won't be so jolly then!

I admit I'm not one of those men who understand things immediately.

I'm not a man who, for example, learns to speak Spanish just so he can order the proper chimichanga at the Taco Teca.

No, knowledge comes to me slowly, but I believe this "slow uptake" and inability to "take the hint" allows true knowledge—gnosis—to eventually infiltrate my being.

It is knowledge beyond my admittedly rather pitiful striving to "understand."

In NOT understanding the Spanish language, for example, I have come to a greater appreciation for Latin culture.

I have forced myself to learn how to decipher supralinguistic cultural clues in order to place my "order" with aplomb and style.

We'll go someday, you and I, to the Taco Teca and I will show you.

You'll see.

In the same way, when I tried/was forced to explain myself to my court-ordered therapist, she, with her beady eyes and piercing beak, asked, after much hemming and hawing, "Did that man touch your penis?"

I laughed.

"Did he?"

For you see, this therapist was such an idiot she needed a direct answer to a direct question, as if that would solve anything!

"Oh yeah," I said then, waving a hand dismissively, because the penis-touching was all so long ago, and I could see the therapist wanted to DEFINE me by this one act, going on and on about "trespass" and "incest," and so on.

Who cares?

Couldn't she see that NOT uncovering the memory, not examining it for clues, leaving it alone in the past, made it all the more interesting?

She wanted to neutralize it!

But why?

Such "traumas" have made me who I am, and I long ago stopped apologizing for who I am.

I don't speak Spanish.

Deal with it.

Bring me a chimichanga!

But my case?

Let's not be distracted by these trifles, and let us concentrate on what does indeed matter.

And what matters?

Truth, my dears; justice, unions, reunions, the coupling of man and woman, boy and girl, father and son, myself and Charli, marriage.

"Marriage," in this case, meaning a "whimsical" "event," developed, it seems, for mere entertainment or, worse, photo opportunities.

Beyond what we both now know to be the true nature of this wedding (a point through which Chris Novtalis will stick his own penis), it makes me sad.

It's as if it's just a party thrown by the couple for their friends and family, marking no real occasion but itself.

A wedding should be a societal ceremony of some kind, not simply a drunken game with a free chicken dinner.

I have been to a similar wedding to what Charli has planned—I have, readers, a nephew.

At his shabby nuptial event, it seemed there was a veritable ocean of twenty-five-year-olds, all dressed "fashionably," sizing one another up, preening.

I am aware that fashion, by its very nature, calls untoward attention to its deviation from normative style, but every single article of clothing worn by these young men and women seemed to either have invisible quotation marks hovering above it or some ridiculous lighted arrow signs mocking the very idea of clothing.

Can no one under thirty simply wear a suit or a dress, get a haircut, or sport a pair of shoes without screaming, "Notice above all that I am special!"?

Don't bother answering.

The question is obviously rhetorical.

And the drinks!

I simply wanted a Michelob Ultra and was told (quite rudely) that there was only a "signature cocktail" made with rum, or a "shandy" made from light beer and lemonade.

A shandy!

Can you believe it?

I nearly came to blows with the bewhiskered bartender, and for what?

My date was not a suitable life-mate anyway, and so I withdrew, taking the Greyhound bus home shortly thereafter.

To see my homely nephew mark the occasion this way was unfortunate, but to see a jewel of femininity like Charli planning such a fête is appalling.

And what, finally, does she have planned?

A reckoning:

1. Nico Novtalis and Charli Vistons are to be consecrated in marriage at the Clark House Inn on June 10, 2009 (the day after tomorrow!).
2. Chris Novtalis, Nico's "brother," the immoderate moderator who has caused trouble from the very start, will (shockingly!) be the best man.
3. The day before the wedding a "family luncheon" will be held, followed by an invitation-only "bachelor/ette party" at this same Clark House Inn.
4. The "family luncheon" and "bachelor/ette party" will feature sushi bars and many liquor "stations," as well as (I can barely type this without vomiting) a 5K run and a "scavenger hunt."
5. Chris Novtalis clearly desires to steal Charli Vistons from Nico.
6. Chris Novtalis is both a morally bankrupt snake and weak-willed dullard who has unjustly exercised his power as moderator of the blog.
7. We know, therefore, that Chris Novtalis desires the marriage in order to secretly and continually violate the bride's sanctity in a fever of filth and oppression while never having to take on any of the responsibilities of a husband or community member.
8. She will simply be in his "harem."
9. Chris Novtalis must be stopped!!!
10. Pitiable Nico will not himself be able to stop this usurpation, and so I, estranged stranger, find myself duty-bound to block the degradation in the only manner still available to me, namely, point X.
11. I will succeed.

Do you doubt these facts?

Are your sweet brains so sodden with the sentimentality of the occasion that you cannot process what sits in front of you?

Don't be a pack of fools!!!

Shall we revisit the wedding blog's comments to examine how I have seen this particular "occasion" unfolding if I am excluded from saving my Charli from irreparable taint?

In the face of "moderation" I admit I grew more strident in my commentary, for I knew that the sands of the hourglass were thinning, that I only had so much time left to reeducate the masses, so I brought out a bit of the heavy artillery of my imagination.

To wit:

May 15, 2009 5:32PM
NICO!: You're going to pick me up from Mom's to take me to the Clark, right?

May 15, 2009 6:27PM
Chris: Yep.

May 15, 2009 6:43PM
NICO!: Awesome. Can't wait to see you, bro! Less than a month!

May 16, 2009 1:17AM
Bob_A: Community!!!!! Can't you see what is happening?!? Can't you see what will most certainly occur if Chris is allowed to continue? To not only attend the wedding, but chauffeur the very groom to the site?! Disaster awaits, I assure you

because I have a gift—sometimes a curse!—and I can see events so clearly in my mind's eye (so, so clearly) . . .

May 16, 2009 1:25AM
Cousin_Kevin: Your "mind's eye" seems like it might be pretty cashed, bud. Why don't you call it a night? Or, better yet, a life?

May 16, 2009 1:26AM
Bob_A: Cashed? As in, "the state of a marijuana receptacle whose contents have been thoroughly exhausted"? Not even close, you wretch! Community! Ignore this "cousin" (who is clearly a "sock puppet" of the abusive and cowardly "moderator" whose threats I have on file, rest assured)! Could a "cashed" eye see this scene play out so clearly? (Here, I'd like you to imagine me poised over my keyboard, knuckles acrack, shoulders thrust back, and then, with gusto, as if I were a Barnum of the Information Age, I pull back the curtain in front of my forehead to reveal my vision):

After checking to make sure the oven is off, the toaster unplugged, and the back door to his "stylish" apartment locked (for you see his mania for control extends to the smallest detail!), Chris Novtalis will, on June 9, 2009, at 8:07AM, drive out to the suburbs to pick Nico up from their mother's drab den of routine conformity.

Together, then, they will start out for the country wedding.

Nico will sleep in the backseat, snoring lightly, waking every hour or so to change the CD on the scuffed purple Discman his father gave him for his fifteenth birthday (choice detail!). Chris will have unrolled the windows as they drift outside of the city, letting the air wash over him. (We know that even in early June, the city still feels as if it could collapse under a freak snow, because everything there in that city, even the smell of the air, seems tentative, overly cautious, politically correct, does it not? Down here, in the country, everything feels as if it has been in bloom for months, yes? Confident! The air sashays! Let's take a breath and fill our lungs with this purity before we continue.

(   )

Nico's mop of dark curly hair will emerge from the comically filthy backseat of Chris's Honda "Civic."

"I've been getting into Mingus lately," Nico will say (see him clicking a new compact disc in place, snapping the lid shut!). "But you have to have generous ears to really, you know, get it."

(Of course we respect Nico for his interest in jazz, but we can only cringe at his manner of speaking about it—"you know," "like," "kind of," and so forth. Oh, how his commentary clangs against my refined sensibility! Does it surprise you, community, that I would call my sensibility refined? Surely it does not, for my sentences contain musical phrases, my paragraphs obbligatos, my arguments tone poems! Do you doubt me? As I sit here typing, I hum and sway. Certainly you too, by your own will or no, hum and sway along with me? Cashed?!?!? never!!!!!)

May 16, 2009 7:15AM
Kate: omg! This guy is soooo out there?! Is he somebody's uncle?

May 16, 2009 7:17AM
Cousin_Kevin: dnftt

May 16, 2009 7:19AM

Bob_A: What's that you say, "Kate"? Out there? Space is the place, my dear! Maestro! Another scene! (The curtain, boys, the curtain! Unleash the forehead!):

In the rearview, Chris will see Nico flash the broad, open-mouthed smile friends used to call "boyish" but now we know looks more like a Trans-Am that has been supplemented with Bondo. That is, rough. Why his parents never allowed him braces is beyond comprehension. That Charli Vistons wants to settle down with Nico surely baffles the best man, chafes his sense of self. But Chris has his plot laid out perfectly. Charli will marry Nico, but Chris will not be denied his due. He will **** her. Soon. Excited, Chris will mash the accelerator with his hoof.

"Nico, why don't you get an iPod?" he will say, lashing out, conspicuous consumer, unwitting marketer for Steven P. Jobs that he is. "It's not like these compact discs are high fidelity."

(Chris's voice is as thin as his character. It is, I imagine, an insufferable baritone that somehow travels through his nose before his mouth, then comes out in a haughty hack. Sickening.)

Nico, bless his heart, will make sea lion–like noises as he settles his bulk down in the backseat. He will (rightly!) dismiss Chris's suggestion with a wave of his hand and begin a reverie.

"I saw a Mingus tribute once," Nico will say in his characteristic mumble. "At the Drake Metro. Right before they played the encore, the saxophone player said, 'This song goes out to the ladies . . . because without the ladies'—it was really funny, he said, 'because without the ladies, we wouldn't be able to have sex!'"

(What a joke! Mingus tribute? No. I admit it is, in fact, my own creation.)

"Hilarious," Chris will deadpan, unappreciative, disapproving of anyone else's pleasure but his own. "Maybe I'll use that as your toast."

Nico will laugh again loudly (sweet boy!), unaware how he has been mildly insulted and "one-upped" by Chris.

"Nice," Nico will say, nestling into his wadded suit jacket and closing his eyes. "That's funny, man. You're funny."

Chris will of course smile his thin-lipped smile at the compliment, for he needs such flattery, he gobbles it insatiably like a dirty cannibal sucking human muscle from a femur bone in some tribal muck.

"Are you still doing the website?" Nico will say with a yawn. "You should write up some wedding toasts and post them."

"Post them?"

"Yeah. To the website."

Chris will here feel a pang of conscience. He will want to explain to Nico that the website has gone horribly astray, that he has mismanaged it to such a degree that shutdown is imminent, that he has failed his friend, his compatriot, his brother, because he is not only secretly in love with the bride but also afraid of the truth and prejudiced against the type of men who speak such truth to power. But no, in the rearview, Chris will see Nico's mouth drooping open and his face going slack. Asleep. Silence.

Here, the moment will present itself that will alter the course not only of this little scene but of all of our lives. Community!!! Pay attention!!!! The blood will be on your hands!!!!!! For observe: A Dodge Neon will here sneak up on Chris and Nico in the right lane. (Chris will, of course, wallow in the left lane as if it were by rights his alone.) This Neon will lumber and swerve. It will be too close. It will trail a noxious gray cloud from its battered exhaust pipe as it nearly runs Chris's Honda "Civic" off the road. The Neon's driver, a robust-looking man with a trim goatee and ruddy complexion, will smile wryly to himself before leaning slightly to the left, and—yes!—clipping the "Civic." It would just be a trifle, but because Chris's instincts have surely been neutered by video game play and sugary cereal, he will feel the contact, swerve left, and then, fatally overcompensating (of course!), he will swerve again back to the right!! His rear right tire will touch the Neon's scuffed bumper (the car will be borrowed); the Civic's rear left tire will buckle under; Nico in the backseat, still half-asleep, will smile faintly as the surge of inertia grips his ******; the car will flip, crash, explode on the interstate with Chris and poor Nico dying in a flurry of snapping bones and sizzling gristle. Screams. Everyone will grieve, though Charli not as much as one might expect. The Neon will drive on into the sunset.
THE END

Oh, dear readers!

It pained me to speak in these voices and to imagine the deaths of two vibrant young people, but I found I could do it so easily!

I found that, for example, Nico's voice erupted from my chest when I simply closed my eyes and imagined myself having been at an early age beaten severely about the head with a baseball bat.

True, I have sat for hours with my two hands acting out scenes between these characters, with my Nico hand (left) drooping down, thumb-chin rolling and lumbering to make simple phrases while the Chris hand (right) poses stiffly with its haughty fingers in the air, waiting its turn to make some pseudointellectual comment in response.

They have a rapport, it's true, and some nights their conversations go on and on in my mind. Acting them out with my hands and then writing out the dialogue is one of the only ways I am able to cleanse my mind of these thoughts, and so I must play out the string.

I know it doesn't work to write it out, that all of this won't leave me just because I make it manifest in language and, for example, post it to the public. I keep it inside of me and its corridors expand accordion-like as I write.

The ideas—and the consequences of the ideas!—become vast and, at the same time, dense, like dark ice spreading over the expanse of my soul. And yet I continue to write, to think, to act, and to communicate, for dear readers, I've been told my examinations of the dark floes illuminate the world for others.

These troubles are not mine alone, and though it often feels, here in the deep night, that I am the only one struck by the cold, it is not so! I have found peers, and through these admirers, or even simple acknowledgers, I find a thaw becomes possible. It does not occur, mind you, but it becomes an object of hope for me. And so I go on, and in some instances, it's true, I act out a scene with my hands or type out the vagaries of a thought with the hope that I will in fact be able to fling it from my mind, as if it were some kind of parasitical crustacean hoping to suction out my essence through my face or mouth.

I fling it out into the world: Begone!

But perhaps I am cursed, for postfling I often find myself unable to quite forget. There was something beautiful in that parasitical purple flesh. Or if not beautiful, at least valuable. To me, or others.

True, there is something of "John Cage" in my imaginings.

No doubt I could make a mint if I were to indulge some ascot-wearing poof at a gallery with my renditions of Chris and Nico's scat. But, you see, I have standards.

I have integrity. My hands are not show ponies. Though it is no real effort to put forth this scene for you, members of the community, it is not *art*.

It is simply a way of both siphoning off the pressure accumulating in my skull from inside and of blowing off the imposition bearing down on my face from outside.

A letting.

I've found that I am inadvertently bridging the gap between otherwise isolated islands of consciousness, providing a service, but my true art, dears, lies elsewhere.

I will reveal only this to you now: it is in the grand American tradition of Eakins, Roth, Poe, Rockwell, and Eastwood.

I am well aware what nonsense the tastemakers put forward today as "art," but I am not fooled.

I know the scam.

They must *pretend* it is art available and accessible to all—for aren't galleries free? museums pay what you wish?—but this is a lie.

Knowing they can't physically block the people, they set up shibboleths, passwords, codes embedded in the work that only the ELITE have had opportunity to learn through their private colleges and grant-funded retreats.

It is a racket, and if one does not know the *passwords,* the ways to talk about "art," then one will be escorted from the premises, the conversation, the milieu, just as swiftly as workers and vagabonds once were escorted from the salons of Europe.

But don't misunderstand me: I know the codes!

It would have been irresponsible of me not to learn them.

It was easy.

Duchamp.

Black women.

Digital reproduction.

But just because one is aware doesn't mean one must endorse!

Don't be a fool!

My art is in constant battle with these forces.

Soon, perchance, I will reveal some of it to you, but until then, a little more of this Left Hand and Right Hand routine?

Would that please you?

Yes?

Well, it seems my mind is full of voices tonight, so let's forget the crash and explosion I presented on the blog. (I admit, I may have gone too far there to make my point that lives are in danger, but I feel justified in my exaggeration, for the community must be made aware!)

Let's instead roust Nico from his slumber in the Honda "Civic" and have these two converse again so we can learn more of their pitiable selves through a dialogue that may in fact reveal more to you than my explanations and comments alone ever could.

Such is even *this* lowly art!

Now, you see, I only have to imagine my hands in conversation again, and the scene arrives.

If I could still comment on the blog, no doubt I would simply post a transcript there, but since I am BANNED, this will be a scene solely for you, my dears!

Note: I need not clutter the vision with excess verbal styling, but rather let it flow directly from my mind's eye to some (as yet unfound) luminous screen.

Of course it's not only this Charli situation that lends itself to such writing! No, ever since this imbroglio started, I've felt as if a fiery belch were constantly about to uncork from deep in my gut. Sadly, no full fiery belch ever quite manages to spring forth, and so at night, after I wake up coughing from the stomach acid burbling up into the back of my throat, I stay awake for hours, doing "yoga," breathing exercises, and obscure gargle remedies in my room, but nothing keeps the surge at bay for long.

Sometimes, true, a belch of some kind does indeed uncork, but then another one reveals itself to be right where the last one had been.

Glorious nature knows how to punish!

Here's a belch now—under my wishbone, in the soft solar plexus, expanding.

Oof!

Of course, I have been to my doctor, who prescribed the generic version of a drug featured in commercials with gray-haired men running to the bathroom in the middle of candlelit dinners with dazzling blondes.

You've seen it—*Ask your doctor about Briostac.*

I did ask my doctor, and I took the medicine, but it only made the fiery belches feel as if they had a ring of ice around them.

Naturally, I told the doctor, and the result was of such interest that I've rendered the scene for you here as, shall we say, an appetizer?

Yes, let's say that.

INT. DOCTOR'S OFFICE. DAY.

[THE DOCTOR stands with a clipboard, nodding, while I sit on the table, clothes off, a gown hanging loosely from my frame, one hand rolling forward in courtly fashion.]

ME
. . . the fiery belches feel, you see, as if they had a ring of ice around them.

DOCTOR
(nonchalant)
Oh yeah. That's a side effect.

ME
Of the Briostac?

DOCTOR
Yep. Or whatever it is you're taking. Generic, right?

[The DOCTOR gestures over at my "Saturday" clothes in a pile by the chair, under the table of insipid magazines.]

DOCTOR
Hey, why don't you prop your elbows up on the table, and I'll see if you've got any black gunk in your butt. Heh.

[Despite the inappropriate strangeness of the DOCTOR's laughter, I do as I'm told.]

DOCTOR
Such a strange feeling.

ME
There are worse things.

DOCTOR

(affronted)

No, I mean for me. Putting a finger up there. Not cool.

[The DOCTOR shudders and unsheathes his hand. He tosses the glove expertly into the biohazard bin. He furiously scrubs both hands in the sink. I turn over.]

DOCTOR

(frowning)

Your kitty's clean. Keep taking the medicine and we'll send you to a specialist in a month if it doesn't clear up.

ME

But the medicine makes it worse!

[The DOCTOR nudges me on the shoulder with his left hand and nods down to his right hand, which is out for me to shake. I shake it.]

DOCTOR

(sliding out the door)

All right. You have a good one!

[I stand in the cold room with my pants off. (Humiliation!) A nurse eventually comes in to shoo me out to the payment desk where the receptionist baffles me with paperwork.]

[FADE TO BLACK]

So you see!

My talent for revelation extends to many genres! Of course, I've been told my work is a bit challenging, that it would take a true *auteur* to fully realize it, but I shall not pander or dumb it down.

Lest you worry about my "condition," you should know I have it under control. I keep a digestion diary, recording everything I eat, how my stomach feels after, and what kind of excremental end point the whole process comes to. There, I am able to read that my condition is improving.

On a camping trip by myself in March, for example, I noted that I had, from morning until midnight, ingested nothing but tamari almonds and red wine.

I fell asleep on a partially inflated air mattress in my tent and awoke just as dawn broke over the hills.

I felt an overwhelming urge pressing at my lower back.

After running into the freezing woods, I unleashed, with an ecstatic grunt, an inverse cast of my large intestine.

I stared at the steaming pile in wonder, then scrambled back through the wet leaves to my tent to record the event in a joyous fever.

That digestive event remains one of my most cherished memories of the past few years; not a birthday, not a vacation, not a party—that big defecation alone has made me happy!

But whom could I share this happiness with?

The last girl I dated, a thirty-five-year-old hussy (who, I should note, misrepresented herself in her online profile to a nearly criminal degree) remained squeamish about digestion issues the whole time we were together, claiming to her perpetual horror that "boys always have to talk about it."

Always one to zig when the boys zagged, I acted very prim when I was first with her.

No bodily conversation, no restroom visits without matches, and thorough wipings of the bowl after urination.

It had become such a *repressed* digestion environment that once, when I hovered over her on her couch, kissing her neck in my patented way, she adjusted her weight and squeaked out the tiniest piff from her digestive tract's end point.

I laughed and told her it was like the sneeze of a rabbit.

Eyes wide in horror, she ran out of the room in shame, thinking I was disgusted at her little explosion.

I realized then that I had perhaps overplayed my hand.

Our relationship ended soon after—for obvious reasons.

Back to the point: I believe in you, dear readers, and I know, since I have recorded "rough cuts" of a few of the "Charli" screenplays whilst playing each part myself, that these scripts are not *unrealizable*.

Looking back on my most recently finished scene—one that I may indeed post for you should anyone express an interest—I am astonished at my facility with the genre.

What a scene! I admit, I have impressed myself.

It's only a matter of time before you see this scene (and the others I have on file!) on screens across the country.

The full-length feature will be called, I think, *The Rapists of a Generation.*

I see David Duchovny playing a certain pivotal role.

But please don't be distracted by this hint of riches!

Come back to me, dear readers!

I have merely mentioned the screenplay to illustrate a point, that the TRUTH is being suppressed.

How do I know these things?

How can I predict the future in this manner?

Is it because I possess a superhuman intellect?

Perhaps.

I have never been given the proper tests, but I believe this genius is simply a product of observation and deduction—and age, of course; it does beget wisdom about some things, despite what you have heard. ☺

Strange, isn't it?

I'm beginning to reclaim all the power now despite what it might look like.

I have nothing, you see.

I am a nobody.

What could this puffed-up somebody possibly do to me that hasn't already been done by countless others?

I'm like the Vietcong, the Sandinistas, the PLO, the American Revolutionaries, while Chris is just a bruise in the side of a dying empire.

A bedsore.

I know.

But it is just those bruises, those bedsores, that will become infected and run with pus and eventually weaken the immune system so that the host will cough his last burbling soon enough.

Yes.

He appears to have everything, but more importantly he believes himself to have everything. Of course that makes him weak.

A name, a job, a reputation, a "family." I have none of these things. But, you see, I will take it all away from him. I will make him into a creature beneath me, so he can feel what it's like, finally, to be shunned.

It does not feel good.

Though I imagine there will be some consolation for him, knowing, as he does, that he deserves his fate.

Will I ever be happy again?

Will I ever feel free of the excruciating burden of this crusade?

It is torture, but I admit it is a kind of exquisite torture for I know I am in the right.

I am like Buster Keaton beset by distracting morons in *The Passionate Plumber.*

I must remain true and keep my eyes closed to the temptations of defeat and appeasement.

He has offered, I admit, appeasement.

Chris has offered to "talk things through" over the phone, but what could he possibly say to me?

That he is sorry?

He could only bewitch me with his sophistry as he has bewitched all the rest.

I refuse.

You see, the real tragedy of my banishment is not personal, but that we were on the cusp of exposing the secret cabal hiding in plain sight, the gentlemen's agreement between powers that, through miraculous circumstances, can be revealed on an admittedly humble wedding blog.

Yes, I'm aware Chris implemented this wedding blog simply out of obligation to follow the fashion, to, in what has become commonplace, coopt an authentic community like the one we had for a time over at BlissfulBasket.com, YoungUns.com, or even AdamsFuneralHome.net.

I don't blame him or any of the other mindless followers!

For what courage would have had to be on display for a man to stand up in his soulless office building, in some gray meeting room, and say, "No! This, at long last, is finally something that is not ours to take!"

Oh, it surely would have caused heads to burst open in wonder, fetid juices splattering over dull paperwork just to have someone acknowledge the unchecked greed underlying all the actions of these organizations; but not just this organization—each and every organization involved, wittingly or no, in this cabal!

They are all in it together!

American capitalism knows how to profit off of a perpetual war machine funded by the state, so instead of cranking up production to meet the war needs, the state cranks up war to meet the production needs!

All throughout the empire, citizens trade their time and energy with the "machine" in exchange for comfort, and so comfort keeps the wars going.

And you all, if you won't stand with me, continue to aid and abet this comfort by colluding in the conspiracy to silence the comfortless!

But, you see, I am standing up where you would not, and, dear me, most likely *could not*.

You have much to lose—or so you think, though in fact I hope you can see that you couldn't be more wrong—whereas I, lonely, bereft, cut asunder by the world, have nothing to lose.

I am offering you my undying loyalty in exchange for what?

Nothing!

A mere acknowledgment that, yes, I exist, that you do in fact hear me, that this isn't all in my mind, that I need not be RESTRICTED IN THIS MANNER!

As you may know, I offered the same to this know-nothing underthing Chris, but he refused me.

In fact, I suspect he hired a vandal to deface my (rented) property in an act of hateful defiance to my overture, for the day I posted a few revelations on the blog, I came home from my grocer rounds to find a fresh egg cracked on the door to my residence.

Can you believe it?

I am still almost unable to type it without flying into a destructive rage—and, in fact, the only thing that keeps me from dashing my brains against the wall is that the vandal wasn't able to penetrate the outer ramparts of the building to defile my actual door, only the front door of the building itself.

To be honest, it was more of the sidewall to the east of the door, but his point was made, the motherless scum!

How could such a lunatic even be allowed near Charli?

It pains me generally but also specifically in my heart's left-most chamber to know he could succeed in his campaign to destroy what could conceivably be a fruitful union.

What concerns me terribly is that Charli has become so acclimated to corruption through our "society" that she would allow Chris to ravish her under the guise of some sort of "open marriage" while Nico fiddles unaware.

The whole thing must be stopped, but I can see that we will allow this "best man" into the wedding, that no one will stop him.

And, most importantly, I will remain excluded, so the event will proceed.

Is it difficult to continue to imagine what might happen even though we have been banned?

No.

We need merely apply the force of our imaginations to the information already gained from Charlico.com/blog.

We know there will be a "family luncheon" and a "bachelor/ette party" at the Inn, so we know the best man will stroll into what the Inn calls its "open-air ballroom" at the tail end of this very luncheon.

We know from viewing the online floor plan that this room at the Clark House Inn is more of a functional storage space than a "ballroom," but why quibble with novice architectural terms?

The space has the requisite ten thousand square feet of hardwood to hold the bar carts, the sushi "stations," and the 107 guests in town for the free drinks, the louche party, the chance to spy some young bridesmaid in a drunken sprawl.

And, of course, the wedding itself.

What a disaster!

When I take time to breathe, to practice my ritual cleansing (I imagine my inhalation bringing the good forces of the outside world into my body through my nostrils, and then I imagine the good forces of my interior world exiting my body through my nostrils upon exhale), I can vividly see in my mind's eye how the wedding will proceed, how Chris will slither his way through the family, partaking in the occasional frottage until he is there by the bride's side as some sort of dance circle forms.

Music from Pink, Beck, Sting, or some other one-named hack will blare. You can hear it, I'm sure.

But can we imagine a proper ending to this scene? Can we imagine one where a certain friend of your narrator finally delivers on a long-ago debt? Let's call him HORACE, and let's open our minds to the possibilities.

EXT. CLARK HOUSE INN. NIGHT.

[HORACE, in a trench coat, stands in the shadows at the edge of the ballroom. In a flash, HORACE raises a rifle from inside his coat and aims first at NICO, then at CHARLI. No one notices. The blissful couple remains unaware, watching in wonder as SOME CHUBBY KID dances in abandon to a gay torch song. The rifle's site first frames CHARLI. Beautiful, she casts her gorgeous hair first in one direction, then the other. The site moves on to NICO—nervous, breathing through his mouth, balling his hands into fists. Then, finally, CHRIS, in contrapposto pose, his arm secretly sneaking around CHARLI's waist, his mouth twisted into a smirk. HORACE steadies the barrel with his left hand. HORACE breathes in.]

HORACE
(quietly to himself)
This one is for you, friend.

[HORACE fires. Outside of the Inn, crows alight from the trees at the sound, which echoes across the valley. CHARLI sees the flash first in her peripheral vision before she feels CHRIS's grip on her waist tighten. His greasy fingers slowly release (though not without a final, fleeting brush across her buttocks!). She looks back and sees the cretin crumpling onto the ballroom floor, his face splattered with what looks to her like clumps of mud. Blood begins to seep from the clumps. CLOSE-UP on CHARLI as she realizes, slowly, that someone has shot CHRIS in his stupid face! She inhales to scream, but before her diaphragm can squeeze out a sound . . .]

HORACE

No time to play nurse!

[HORACE has bounded over from the party's edge to grip her by the hair (Brutal, but what can we do? The same nature that will allow HORACE to shoot CHRIS is the same that causes him to roughhouse). CHARLI's scalp burns in pinpricked points at first, then all over her head. HORACE pulls her by her hair away from NICO and the rest of the party, and as she stumbles along with him she finds herself concentrating on the RC Cola machine flickering near the main entrance, wondering what will become of her life now that she is free of CHRIS and NICO. HORACE pulls her into the darkness.]

[FADE TO BLACK]

Grim, I admit. In fact, it's a movie not unlike those I suffered through a decade ago when I spent so many nights at the cinematheque, standing sentinel for another young beauty beset by deluded aggressors.

But let's not digress.

I know I sound tough, strident, at peace with my convictions, but it does wear on me, I admit it. It is the most tiresome cliché, but it is nonetheless true in this case: no one understands me.

Even as an ungainly youth I was perplexed at how my teachers and "betters" made connections with so many of my peers, and yet all of these elders steadfastly refused to "get" me or acknowledge my exceptionality. But what is there to "get"? Who am I? Am I so special? Should I have, in the end, changed who "I" was just to be "got" by the knuckleheaded throng surrounding me?

I'm sure your superficial answer is a resounding "no," as it has been from the mouths of whomever I've asked. But of course you are a hypocrite!

When pressed to the point, you all ask me to change, to conform, to give up my essential self to fit in with the lumpen bureaucratariot! Once again, I refuse!

This must make me unhappy, yes?

Of course this is the conclusion most people draw when they dimly perceive the outlines of my existence, but here is the strange thing: I am happy! Joyous, even!

It is the conformist, the socialite, the wedding attendee, the one who goes along only to sacrifice everything worth going along for, who is unhappy!

I have no burdens on my conscience.

I enjoy my meager meals.

I sleep soundly, when I choose to sleep.

I read.

I listen to Archie Shepp.

It is, as a matter of fact, a quite lonely existence, except for these facts:

1. I have been wronged.

2. I am right.

So, yes, I am frustrated.

I am bewildered.

I am angry.

But I am not unhappy.

I have my integrity, and I have my grievances.

But I require no pity from you.

I merely require justice!

And it is this requirement that prods me to go deeper, faster, to push on into the untamed wilds of my gift, to breach the next layer of consciousness in this charade, and to do so without the inhibitions I have heretofore indulged—off with this constricting shirt!

Let the sweat roll down my sides unimpeded!!!

Isn't it natural?

Why, I'll go barefoot!

Yes!

Let's not be afraid of the truth, my dears!

Let's let our primal instincts take over!

True, we have seen that Chris's physical threat to Charli will be nullified by my proxy at the event itself, and so, you may ask, "Why continue writing when you have a plan of action?"

Because, don't you see, the existential danger still looms!

For Nico.

For Charli.

For us.

The *mentality* Chris engenders has already begun to corrupt us from inside, to hem us in, to cause us to *censor ourselves*.

Oh, it burns!

How could we have allowed him to affect us so?

Make no mistake: he has affected us.

We are not clean.

We are cramped and filthy still.

Off with the pants!

We are, in some ways, behaving worse than Chris!

And is that not his ultimate victory?

Here I feel the guilt, and, yes, shame come creeping, and so I must keep typing in order to evacuate the demons from my soul!

It is of the utmost importance that we battle the forces of oppression with our conjoined imaginations in whatever form the muse allows, but I sense that we won't be able to fully appreciate this oppression without first digging into that loamy humus where we might begin separating the tangled roots of love, desire, loathing, and, I admit it, self-delusion that make up my formative years.

MFL.

Again, MFL!

This was well before the advent of blogs, dear readers, and before I had truly accepted my role as an outsider, so it was a different world, one in which I had to employ a very different set of skills to keep track of my interests.

Let me explain, and in explaining, let me pull you back to another world, another place, and another time: 1989.

Yes, in 1989 I was enrolled in a "work-study" scholarship program with the food services department of the state school all the spoiled children of engorged magnates continue to use as a fallback when their plans for received aristocracy fall through.

There, in Creosotte Dining Hall, surrounded by imbecilic frat boys and airheaded candy stripers, I ran the soft serve stand on weekday mornings.

As per the instructions delivered to me by a hirsute woman of dubious extraction, I kept the cafeteria's cabinets full of sprinkles, and I kept the whirring soft serve machine's various parts in working order using a certain jellied lubricant and scrub brush.

This was no small feat when every young coed desperately and continually needed "a chocolate one, pleeeze," though I was (and am!) an efficient enough worker to make enough time for supra–soft serve observations of my peers.

Yes, I had to wear a silly paper hat, but more to the point: I first observed MFL (whom I will now, in this public space, for legal reasons, call "Rachil"), the inaugural morning of the school year in that Indian summer of 1989, a time when the "punks" all still wore leather, and the cars were all still Japanese made.

And a beauty like Rachil did not go in for "Prince."

At least not when I first met her.

No, she looked like a young Ally Sheedy, an untouched Ally, an Ally waiting for initiation into the older Ally world.

She liked her soft serve extra soft.

MFL. Immediately, it was so.

I soon learned that "Rachil" worked as a ticket seller at the newly opened University Cinematheque on East campus, and, it happened that I received a school employee discount at this very same University Cinematheque.

I quickly became the Cinematheque's most loyal patron, suffering through all the films twenty-year-olds now consider "cult classics" simply so I could have a brief minute of face-to-face interaction with MFL.

I might have been her MFL, if only I had been given the proper chance.

Who can say? The past is passed.

What we can say is that our eyes often met during the ticket transaction, and one time she did indeed touch the side of my hand with her ring finger.

I felt a spark.

But, we'll never know what could have been, because mine enemy (whom I will call from here on out for the very same legal reasons "Corn") also worked there at the Cinematheque, running the projector from a little dank hovel.

Even from where I sat in the front row, I could often hear him guffawing his way through the films at the back of the cinema.

The soul may indeed grow in darkness, but one must consider which particular soul this is before one registers the fact as a positive or negative occurrence!

Worse still, Corn could often be found hovering outside the ticket booth, practically licking the glass that protected poor Rachil from just such "flirtations."

He would stand idly by while she attempted to do her job, horning in on the time that was by rights the customers' in order to continue some fatuous discussion of Jay McInerney or Norman Mailer (Corn fancied himself an "intellectual").

Isn't it ironical that the cinema was the smithy of their base ingratitude and that my secret screenplay forecasts their future manifestations' eventual downfall?

Yes.

It is.

Let's enjoy the irony for a moment.

Perhaps in due time I will post the entirety of my as-yet-unproduced screenplay for your enjoyment, dear readers, but until then let's acknowledge that the screenplay form, glorious as it is in my hands, has its limits.

It cannot encompass all of experience.

If we are to fully understand these types of relationships, which we are indeed to do if we are to proceed, then we need to push beyond all "genre" limitations.

Yes, it is obvious that the past requires a novelist's touch, that majestic sentences must stream from the pinpricks of facts to adequately capture the time and place of my (or any!) sentimental education, for the novelist takes a true story and lies about it, or takes a lie and tells a true story about it. Either way, to the reader it all appears at the same time to be gospel and supreme artifice.

Shall we begin?

CHAPTER 1

Rachil sold tickets in a brightly lit glass-enclosed booth that sat in front of the shabby University cinema, which itself fit snugly inside a student union, a campus hub at the center of a tawdry rural town made nationally prominent only by this second-rate educational institution's rah-rah football team.

Seen from above, the campus looked like a metastasizing cancer growth in an otherwise robust body of farmland.

A boy named Corn ran the cinema's projector in a dark concrete room that smelled like wet Band-Aids and trench foot.

It was 1989.

Night after night, Corn would curl his lithe body around the film splicer, snipping out the stills of titillating scenes for his "private collection," sweat pouring from his greasy scalp as his wormy fingers did their wormy work.

Night after night, Rachil, an almond-eyed brunette with the dark allure of a young Ally Sheedy, would sell her allotment of tickets and, drawn by a rank impulse quite inexplicable, would knock on the fireproof door to the projection booth while Corn built up or broke down the film.

He would heave open the door and bid her enter with a pervy grin.

Up she would climb, mounting the few steps to the projection platform where Corn sat amid the fluttering reels of celluloid.

On some nights, as Rachil and Corn lounged in that dark bunker, he would watch her laugh her perfect laugh and wonder how he hadn't always known about the blaring clown horn that existed inside of him.

It now blared all day long: *RAAAACHHHHILLLL RAAAACH-HHHILLLL!*

Yes, it was the horn of love, readers. We can almost pity poor Corn.

Before this horn, Corn had merely expelled his seed into/onto whatever deluded virgin crossed his path without a care for "feelings," but now, there *she* was, leaning on the steel banister on the stairs of the projection room, rolling her eyes as she recounted tales of barroom boys with earnest ardor, and suddenly the horn sounded in Corn's heart:

RAAAAAAACHHHHILLLLL!

It rendered him glassy-eyed and mute and, yes, full of feelings.

"What a dork!" Rachil would say of a recent beau, chewing a pinky nail, settling onto the projection room floor cross-legged.

"Totally," Corn would say, in a patently false imitation of the argot of the day, willing to give up everything, including his very way of speaking, to stay in her presence. "Can't these morons see that it's much more fun to be free of 'relationships' and all their, like, entrapments?"

"I *know*," she would say.

"I mean," he would say, "they could be like us, right? *Best* friends!"

"Sex," she would say, idly plucking an eyelash. "Yuck."

He would smile his secret smile to himself and hunch over to hide his bourgeoning "member."

Corn could hardly believe no one else heard all this honking in his heart, that no one could see the falseness of his every move nor understand that his canny claim of interest in her life was simply a screen for his true lustful urges.

But no one could, it seemed, so he nearly pulled off his plot to enslave Rachil sexually, but enter a sad Percival who blithely lurched along the campus paths, his own heart honking the same sad tune.

No, dear readers, not me!

Don't be silly!

It was, yes, Corn's lumbering, wayward childhood chum, who we will for legal reasons here call "Rico."

Rico disrupted Corn's penetrating line!

Rico would, on these very same nights, drag his boot-heels along the leaf-strewn paths of the campus, humming tuneless tunes, thinking of Jesus.

How do I know these things?

Patience, dear readers, patience—all will be revealed in due time.

But perhaps a true novel would present something of its narrator at this point?

Should we have had a preface or a prologue, something indicating that this "I" construct existed somewhere first as pure thought, as a formal "Point X"?

But then that this "I" was slowly pinched into the world, unborn from reality into this farce?

I remember darkness, shadows, fingers, and hands.

When I was a child I was treated as a child, and so I left that child behind.

Even before I left, I was no longer there.

CHAPTER 2

Night.

Summer.

Corn and Rachil were at the dark biker bar where they had begun spending their after-hours, "alone together" to borrow a phrase.

The biker bar was Corn's idea, a futile attempt to prove to Rachil that he was a "stud," though he was secretly terrified some leather-bound pituitary case would test his manhood by running a swarthy hand over Rachil's supple body, his lust-crazed eyes daring Corn to "do something" as his fingers probed and pinched.

Corn worried, too, that perhaps secretly Rachil would enjoy such pinches and would rut with a biker on the pool table in front of everyone while he stood impotently by.

On this particular fateful night, in the midst of these puerile thoughts, he watched Rachil skip off to fetch more beer at the bar, leaving Corn by himself in the shabby booth where, alone for more than a minute with his paranoid thoughts, he became restless.

There was a swarthy fellow near the pinball machine.

Would he be the one?

Damnit! Where had Rachil gone? Where was his beer?

Not only was he paranoid, but he required service!

Corn made a sour face and turned toward the bar, and there—oh there at the nicked and worn bar of the Boiler Room—he saw her.

What was this!?!?

He saw *his* Rachil, *his* point B, shamelessly flirting with some hulk with his back turned!

The hulk sported an incongruous floral-print shirt and a tattered cowboy hat.

Who was this usurper at the bar who caused Corn's love to laugh uproariously at some joke?

She placed a hand on the floral-print chest and gave a playful push.

An unexpectedly powerful horn crept slowly up Corn's spine, engulfing his skull and blaring out through his eyes *RAAAAACHHHHILLLLL!!!!!*

He gritted his teeth.

He got up.

"You!" Rachil said, peering around the hulk as Corn approached, laughing, hugging Corn, her bare arms sliding behind his neck with a strange supple grace.

She kissed Corn's cheek.

That had never happened before.

"Look who's here!" she said, waving a bangled arm toward the hulk, who turned.

Corn shuddered as his eyes met the gaze of the other.

It was, yes, his former "best bud" Rico, who had become so different in only a semester.

Some background about their childhood friendship: it was always thus, Corn the domineering little Caesar to Rico's doughy centurion.

But here at the University, after they had drifted apart in their respective premajors, Rico had finally managed to wriggle out from under his "friend"'s thumb after what were no doubt awkward high school years, a time we need not account for in detail because it is all the same for boys.

Lust.

Shame.

Some graffiti scrawled in marker.

The maw of a slavering beast pressed down on one's privates.

In fact, Rico had begun to finally come into his own at this second-rate school, away from home and Corn's constant presence—he even said a polite hello to the cafeteria help from time to time!

His interests?

Engineering, club sports, Bible study, sobriety, a style of dress in a vaguely "natural" fashion, hacky sack, the Violent Femmes.

"Howdy!" Rico said to Corn in a most disrespectful manner. "Long time no see, bud. How's the movie business?"

Howdy? Corn thought, disgusted. Has he, in the short time since we arrived here, embraced this outlaw lifestyle like some filthy hillbilly? I judge.

"You guys!" Rachil said with a smile. "*Boy* friends!"

Rachil squeezed Rico's arm with both hands then skipped off to the restroom, leaving Corn with this cowboy-hatted peer.

A facing C with no B.

There was an awkward silence.

CHAPTER 3

"Wanna play some sack?" the doughy face under the hat finally asked.

Corn did *not* want to play some sack, but neither did he want to skulk away to the booth defeated in his attempts to impress Rachil, so, outside the bar, he soon found the dusty knit hacky sack bouncing off his chest.

Corn looked as if he were struggling to dance along with bad balalaika music—squatting, kicking the sack up with his instep, then hitting it with his forehead so it lurched halfway back across the circle before landing dead center with a crusty plop.

The faces in the circle did not smile for these strangers, knew what kind of degenerate had entered their midst.

They radiated judgment.

"So I should tell you," Rico said, kicking up the sack with a fluid motion, stalling it on top of his foot, then flicking it over to his left foot and stalling it again (bravo!). "I'm not going to go *all the way* until I'm married, so you don't have to worry about me and Rachil."

He kicked the sack expertly over to a young man with an inexplicable Afro.

"That separates me from the rest of the pack here," Rico said with a jerk of his thumb, "and some people can't handle that. But you know it's important to my faith—Southern Bap."

He leveled a serious look at Corn.

Corn noticed, suddenly seeing his friend afresh, that Rico's eyelashes were ridiculously long and that one of his eyes was still . . . off.

(*RAAAACHHHHILLLLL!!!* We can almost hear the desperate grinding of Corn's molars.)

The sack once again bounced off Corn's chest and landed at his feet.

"Earth to bro!"

A skinny kid in a faded T-shirt stifled a laugh.

Corn picked up the sack and threw it into the bushes like a petulant child.

"Not cool!" the skinny one said, running after the bag.

"Whoop," Rico said, checking his watch. "Gotta go! Bible study at seven. Nice to see you, bub. Really nice. Say bye to Rachil for me. Later."

Rico took off his hat and bowed, curly black hair falling around his puffed face.

Then, he turned and ran with rigid posture toward campus.

Corn watched the flip-flops flap against Rico's mud-smudged heels.

He turned back to the circle, which had closed itself.

He narrowed his eyes and rubbed his hands together.

He would have her . . . somehow!

*

Before we delve into the next chapter of this expertly crafted narrative, dear readers (Are you jealous, Mailer?!?!), let's linger for a moment on the issue of Rico's faith.

It is not simply a work of my imagination.

Of course, it is not how I was raised, and at the time it was more than a bit strange, but I do not judge matters of faith and I advise you to also reserve judgment.

Why?

I'll tell you.

No one can doubt the end-times are near, and so any acquaintance with Scripture (no matter how egregiously presented) will surely help ground a person in the gravity of this apocalyptic interlude.

True, I must appear to you light, carefree, jovial, and playful with my "scenes" and my "witticisms," but make no mistake: blood will flow.

And soon!

I can see it.

If not by the hand of the "Lord," then by a worldwide shift in consciousness that will cause the higher beings among us to cull the litter of frauds and ninnies, charlatans and hustlers.

One day you'll be sitting there in your apartment, reader, idly watching some yuppie walk his Italian greyhound along the primrose path, and as he bends down to grip the greyhound's feces with his plastic-sheathed hand, he will suddenly see, there on the horizon, the first signs of the Event.

The clouds will have turned green, and the leaves on all the trees will quiver with their light undersides exposed.

A blast of cold wind will blow the yuppie's hair back; the Italian greyhound will whimper and scurry behind his master's legs.

First one wayward robin will fly by—too close!

Then another.

A third.

A fourth.

The yuppie's heart will race.

A sharp inhale and then: the deluge!

He is suddenly surrounded by flapping darkness as thousands, perhaps millions of robins, their innate sense of direction exploded by cell phone radiation, pour from the trees down the street like coal through a chute, their fat bodies covering the cars, their white-circled eyes gone insane.

Everything within your vision there at your window will be covered by red breasts and dusty feathers, a pandemonium of wings, claws, beaks, and the sharp pins of feathers nicking and scratching and gouging against the glass—what a terrifying noise!—and surely the man and his dog . . . blood . . . fur . . . flesh.

The dog is dead.

The yuppie is dead.

Just two victims in the worldwide catastrophe.

You will run for cover, but where?

The birds have already begun to make their way in through every available crack in your domicile.

The world has suddenly gone dark.

Cowering in the pantry, you will feel the sound before you really hear it, the maniacal freight train that precedes the tornado.

Close your eyes!

All there will be is the whirring of wings and hellish squawks surrounding you.

Yes, it will be time to die . . .

Politically, of course, corporate democracy cannot stand, and the socialist Big Brother equally appears (to any observant eye) ready to topple, so all it will take is one slight push in either direction for the New World to emerge.

Is this not the prophesied apocalypse?

Where will you be when it occurs, dear readers?

What side of the wall will you be on?

On the side of the People, or on the side of the (so-called) Elites?

Choose wisely!

Do you really want to be sitting in your apartment watching an Italian greyhound defecate without having done your part for justice and righteousness?

Who knows what your last thought will be—most likely some idle lyric from a Roxette song or some such cultural detritus—but there is a chance it will be, "Why did I allow that man's banishment?"

Your soul will sit before ultimate judgment.

CHAPTER 4

After seeing Rico and Rachil together that first time, Corn spent the next few weeks acting as if everything were "normal," as if his entire being didn't hinge on whether or not Rachil came into his concrete bunker to make fun of poor Rico, or to say the date with Rico was dumb, that Rico was a jerk, that the next date would never happen, or that Rico Rico Rico Rico Rico.

Rico!

Corn wanted to kill him, even more now than when they were teenagers together in the drab suburbs.

Despite all that was so clearly wrong about Rico—his lumbering idiocy, his sincerity, his slovenly carriage—Rachil kept going steady with him!

Insane!

Corn plotted Rico's demise in the foul projection booth while the reels of film spun in the darkness.

"Maybe I should just lose it to him," Rachil said one evening, flicking her shy lashes up at Corn, driving him to frenzy there in the dark. "My virginity," she said. "No big whoop."

Corn dropped the top reel from the projector, and the sprocket ripped a two-foot tear in the print of *Batman*.

First off, he thought, she was a virgin?

Innocence perplexed him.

Second, lose it?

To Rico?

Virginity *in play*?

Rachil went out to calm the enraged film crowd in the theater while that incompetent spliced everything back together with shaky hands in the booth.

Popcorn and Jujubes filled the air, catcalls and hoots.

"Is everything okay?" she asked upon her return, eyeing the reel wobbling on the rickety projector.

The Joker had suddenly become a blob of darkness, then switched back again in a yellow streak.

Corn didn't notice, for he was a sloppy, horrid worker who didn't really care about film, only a paycheck.

I can attest to the fact that the crowd took notice, and that the manager was notified.

A soda splashed against the booth door, followed by a shouted obscenity.

Within, Corn was at a loss.

"So when . . . you and . . . heh . . . some date, huh?"

"Let's talk, Corn. I'll be at the Boiler Room," Rachil said. "Gotta meet Rico."

She made a sour face, and left poor Corn in the booth to think over Rico pumping his hips and Rachil moaning in ecstasy with her hands clawing at his floral shirt while he whooped like a broncobuster.

Southern Bap, Corn thought, alone again, gnashing his teeth. Hippy!

We can imagine this is the moment his deepest plot began to hatch like a nest of roach babies in his mind.

He *would* have her, someway, somehow, even if it took years!

(Screenplay adaptation note: acquire rights to Lou Reed's "Walk on the Wild Side.")

CHAPTER 5

Shortly thereafter, Corn took up in the spare room of an old makeshift "church" at the edge of town where Rico resided.

It was stage 1 of his plan.

Most students lived in the dormitories or the fraternities, of course, but Rico, once his "hippy" phase began in earnest, professed an inability to live in such "hives." He set out for the poorer neighborhoods on the outskirts, where tract homes became "churches" and "churches" became bohemian squats.

Poor and bumbling, though, Rico couldn't make do in a "squat" or make rent by himself, even in a nearly abandoned old church in the black part of town, where neither the paperboy nor the pizza guy dared to tread.

So Corn joined Rico at the former Full Gospel Tabernacle, ostensibly to ease his friend's financial burden and to be "friendly," but we know it was, in fact, to ingratiate himself with the frequent visitor, Rachil, whom Corn obsessed over day and night.

*

A note about the "church": on its east side, there was a wall of privet and scrub that presented a problem.

It blocked my view to everything.

A hand-lettered sign in the neighbor's window read "No Trustpassing. Will Call Police."

Obviously, I ignored this empty threat and assumed these illiterate residents would present no impediment if I decided to set up camp there, but in the end the privet proved too dense.

The rampant invasive plant species swarmed east to west, away from this neighbor and around the church, falling away as the red dirt driveway met the other neighbors to the west.

These western neighbors, I deduced, might actually be problematic since they were seemingly *always* outside, though the vantage from the west side was optimal enough to risk it.

A two-beam fence stood in the clearing where the two properties touched, and just beyond the fence sat the three-bedroom house, lorded over by an old woman everyone called Mamma.

Every morning when I left my spot just west of the church, in the deep privet behind the driveway, I saw Mamma ambling around her yard with a bandanna on her head and a full plug of tobacco in her lip.

She waved at me and talked her talk, but I never could understand anything she said.

Good God, her house flooded over—sons, daughters, grandsons, granddaughters, cousins, second cousins, aunts, uncles, and friends—so many that they spilled out into the driveway and onto the fence, even in the early mornings or late nights when I would make my way to the windows.

Rick, Rat, Frank James, Trina, Carbox, Willie, Deidre, Prika, Cedric, Toni, Nanez, Tater, and, every once in a while, twin cousins named Chad and Sam, all teetering on the fence, waving at me, speaking.

Shut up, damn you! My work is done in silence!

Years before Corn and Rico lived in the church, some wayward soul had placed a black metal sign in front of the building's white double doors that, though rusted, still read "Full Gospel Tabernacle" in white letters.

By the time of my approach, the black sign and the white double doors were the only clues that the place was any different from the rows of tract homes down the street, leading into the projects people called—ironically?—the Estates.

Otherwise, it looked like any other dump in the neighborhood, except for the fact that a couple of "crackers" lived there.

Inside the church, the structure still showed traces of "Full Gospel," but the nave had been partitioned off, the transepts cleared into a living room, and the chancel made into a stage, where, in place of a pulpit, Rico and Corn had put a drum kit, two "keyboards," three guitars, two amps, a bass, a saxophone, and a clarinet.

Some nights they would make an infernal racket late into the night, the neighbors in ecstatic communion, wailing away on the clarinet or stomping out a hambone rhythm on the church floor.

Occasionally, Rachil sat there, agog on the tattered sofa, trying to express something besides horror at these strangled attempts at "music."

Corn, for his part, played music constantly, day and night, though I noticed he played two distinct types of music: other people's songs out there on the "stage," Bo Diddley and Deep Purple covers, while in his room, on a guitar he had apparently bought off some poor widow at an estate sale—a 1954 Silvertone with a small American flag Scotch-taped to the body, ridges worn into the fret board, bloodstains on the tuning pegs—he sang his own songs.

These songs had no hambone.

He recorded them on a shabby four-track held together with, one assumes, rubber bands and chewing gum, but I noticed he never played *these songs* for anyone else, just recorded and rerecorded them on the rickety machine in his room.

He sang and sang, but, dear readers, his voice was so terrible!

Like a gassy internal organ compressed by crab claws.

And of course his songs were all about Rachil—maudlin laments of unrequited love and heartache, about a beautiful girl in love with the sad singer's hippy friend.

They recalled the sounds of mewling kittens stuck in a cavernous smokestack.

The whole episode reminds me of another, much less intensely laughable story from my own time as a budding teenager, when I spent my afternoons with my two "friends," Daniel and Emmett.

It is a bit of a digression, but such a story might give you a glimpse into why I knew exactly what Corn was up to.

This way I can express myself without having to blather on in some sordid confessional mode, or worse, attempt to compose some horrid, pathologically sensitive lullaby like Corn himself did, so yes, I will allow myself the indulgence.

You see, Emmett had a sister.

Isn't that how all love stories begin?

She was older, and quite large.

Emmett, Daniel, and I would watch TV and play card games in the basement "rumpus room" of Emmett's house deep in the "swank" part of town, while his sister, Parissa, would have tea with her raggedy girlfriends upstairs.

I don't think it's possible for you to comprehend how strange it was to be Persian, as Emmett and Parissa were, in such a time and place, twenty-five years ago in our semirural township, and so just the fact of being at their house was for us, their peers, an admission of some defect on all of our parts.

We had clearly failed at normal company.

While Parissa and her friends pretended nothing was out of the ordinary upstairs—they talked about boys and schoolwork like the rest of high school feminine society, as if there weren't a dark stink hanging over them, an unacknowledged otherness—downstairs we made no such pretenses.

Our otherness was manifest.

Daniel, "Emmett" (real name: Omar), and I popped zits on one another, burped, gave one another bloody noses, exchanged wadded-up photos and filthy stories, drank concoctions of Schnapps and cough syrup while barely turning our backs to "jack off" into socks.

Every few hours one of us would scramble up out of the basement and cause the girls to shriek, either by spewing soda at them, wagging a discolored penis, or unleashing some form of unholy bodily gas.

We were putrid little pukes, I admit it.

My only saving grace was that I hated Emmett and Daniel, and I hated what I became with them.

I often would sneak into the bathroom to gouge the inside of my thigh with a paperclip as punishment for being there.

But it was worth it.

Why?

Because of Parissa.

Parissa, with her beefy thighs and ponderous cheeks, her dark obtrusive hairs and little feet, her cumin and proto-Rachil/proto-Charli smell, her husky laugh gargling in the fat of her throat, her secret delight in our disgusting attention.

You see, I would debase myself with Daniel and Emmett for as long as it took, until all of Parissa's friends had gone home and she had showered off her plump haunches and globes (a nighttime showerer, up and at school in morning grease and fume), swaddled herself in a robe, and toddled off to her bedroom in the converted basement.

Then, I would feign a yawn, excuse myself from the puerile company I had been keeping.

They would of course stop belching on each other only long enough to give me a good-bye salute of buttocks and a grunted farewell as I pretended to start on my way home.

But I would not walk home!

I would merely slip around to the side of the house and lower myself onto my belly in the cool grass.

Peering over the window well, I could see—just barely—into Parissa's cramped basement room, where she had most often installed herself like a gibbous moon into a chair to listen to a record or read a book.

Oh what a delight just to watch such a fat girl finally free herself of self-consciousness and let it all hang!

Some nights she'd do leg exercises, scratch her ham-like calf, brush her hair, pick at her elbow . . .

Of course I dreamed that one of these nights she would stop inspecting her toenails and begin to lightly trace her fingers across her mammoth belly, plunge a puffy hand into the darkness below to rub out the secret passion (for me!) in a squirmy fit of muffled grunts and sighs.

Alas.

I never saw if she did, for after a few months I was caught.

One night as I lay there prone on the dewy herbe, my chin resting on folded hands as Parissa looped her index finger into the back panel of her underwear and with a deft flick sprung the center cloth loose from captivity between her luscious buttocks—what wonders was I in store for next?—I felt a snide little push on my shoulder.

And there, towering over me, was Emmett, cigarette cupped to the inside, cat-that-got-the-canary look on his stupid face.

"Well, well," he said like the dumb sociopath he was. "Are you looking at my sister?"

"No," I said, as if I could deny it, to simply erase what was happening with a word.

The absurdity of such a patently false statement did not fluster Emmett.

"Five bucks," he said.

"What?"

"Five bucks and I don't tell. I let you keep looking. No problem."

You see?

Do you see what kind of wretched personality I was forced to accommodate?

A pimp!

Far better to be alone, but you can sympathize with a poor adolescent wanting some kind of companionship, can't you?

I wouldn't pay, of course, and so Emmett bolted down the stairs to Parissa's room as I looked on in horror through the window.

I suppose I didn't believe he would actually do it, nor did I believe if I had simply run away she would think him a crazy nuisance and a liar.

Foolishly, I looked on while he burst in and pointed out the window at me.

She, wild-eyed, covered herself up and gaped at the darkness without comprehending—until he flicked the light switch off.

Then I heard her scream (and him laugh).

If she had not been startled and handled so rudely by her brother, do you think she would have found my attention quite so unflattering?

There couldn't have been many boys—if any at all, honestly—who found her as alluring as I did.

You might expect, as I admit I did, sitting there in the dark watching her turn her gaze toward me in horror, that she would appreciate the attention.

Perhaps, under different circumstances, she would have, but Emmett made it so that our great love could never enter the world.

I was banned from the house and ridiculed further at school as a peep.

So you see?

My love has been thwarted from the start.

I could tell you so many more stories, but why pay so much attention to these admitted travesties when for all intents and purposes they are out my control?

I know.

Believe me, I do.

But I've realized a certain vital part of me refuses to accept injustice on whatever scale.

Chris Novtalis, this corrupt dribble of afterbirth, should not be allowed to shut me out.

He should not have the authority, in, yes, the exact same way—the exact!—that the president has not earned the right to make his decisions.

He obviously does not know the lay of the land, is in over his head, and yet he refuses to acknowledge these facts, and by withholding this information, by stonewalling his petitioners, he is making the catastrophe worse.

During the campaign, he listened.

When someone brought up a problem—and there were many, we were helpful!—he addressed it forthrightly.

It was an open and vital conversation in which very serious issues were being discussed, and many problems solved.

But now that campaign, and that discussion, is at zero.

There is nothing.

And, I'm sure you see, that is the very same case on the wedding blog.

Nothing is happening!

It is a barren stretch of white waste.

We are not being heard!

Only the sanitized voices beholden to the established interests get a say!

I truly thought the site would be different.

I should have known, but for a joyous spring—the wild time of innocent youth and happiness—we had a voice, a space, and look at the magnificent work we did.

The proof is there in the record, but before examining the record further—I'm sorry; I've let this digression proceed too far—let us not leave that campus of long ago.

There is more!

Of course now it seems so obvious to say that era was the end of something rather than the beginning, but back then, the thrill felt curiously like hope.

I, for one, believed in my vision of new days with my new love by my side.

These days spread out before me—a completely different time of understanding and empathy was heralded by our reconciliation.

Well, "reconciliation" is perhaps not quite the right word since that does imply a mutual act, when in this particular instance I alone did the reconciling, or, rather, pursued my love object with fervor, so in some ways it was an inverse reconciliation, a natural falling away of boundaries.

I remember when I first saw Rachil truly see me, there in the ticket window with her Louise Brooks bob, sighing, unaware exactly who it was receiving the "employee" discount despite having left his ID at home once again.

She took me in with her almond eyes, up and down, then raised her delicately plucked eyebrows as if to say, "Well, well, you do indeed exist after all!"

I tilted my chin at her, not wanting to overplay my hand, and gave her a wink.

She feigned disgust.

The point: I had finally made contact with my love and it seemed no coincidence that the cinema played host that quarter to films by the new auteurs, those filmmakers we all thought were harbingers of a revolution, but were, in fact, only the end of an evolutionary cycle.

After this showing of *Born on the Fourth of July*, in a daze, I followed (at a discreet distance) Corn and Rachil back to the "church."

I should explain here, dear readers, that I had not yet been permanently cast out of the university at this particular juncture, but had simply been "AWOL," a mysterious absence from the classroom.

I had hoped for a glorious return.

The misunderstanding had yet to occur.

Can I help what others perceive?

Tell me truly, dear readers: is it my fault what goes on in the minds of others?

Surely not, you say, and yet here I sit in my humid room, unloved, cast aside, neglected, and banned, because other members of society cannot perceive my intentions and thus judge my actions correctly.

Incorrectly?

Whatever.

Language fails.

I reach for my tea and hope to find succor, but it is bitter.

How I wish I could still smoke—but in this I believe the doctor might be correct.

But then!

Back then!

I would squat in the shrubs outside the church, smoking cigarette after cigarette, listening through the window to the conversations between Rico and Corn, Rachil and Rico, Corn and Rachil.

I spied the dark dimples forming the small of Rachil's back as she scooped a Spree candy wrapper off the floor of the church.

"You guys," she laughed. "Spree!"

We three—Rico, Corn, and I—swooned.

She had us all in the palm of her hand, and Rico and I were such naïve fools that we thought she and Corn flirted innocently!

It would be the last time I underestimated his powers.

CHAPTER 6

I let myself in through the church window when I thought no one was home, and I sat at the kitchen table smoking one of Rico's menthol cigarettes, pondering the wood paneling on the wall opposite.

One particular eddy had a striking resemblance to the curve of Rachil's neck, and the longer I stared, the more I seemed to see her eyes there, and before long, it was as if I could hear her voice, slightly muffled, almost moaning.

I shook my head to clear it of these sounds—not again!—but I found that no amount of shaking stopped what did indeed sound like moaning.

One of the neighbor kids suddenly burst in.

He wanted to use the bathroom because, he told me, somebody had "torn it up" in the bathroom at his house.

No way was he going in there, he said, no way.

Fine, I waved him over and nodded my approval.

He ran down the hall to the bathroom, but just as quickly he was back.

"I can't get in," he yelled, pointing maniacally back down the hall. "They in there hunchin'!"

"Who's hunchin' what?" I asked with a cough, perplexed by the child's native slang.

"Your boy! He in there hunchin'!"

Since I seemed to have the run of the place, the child evidently assumed some "your boy" relationship between myself and Corn.

It did not seem the time to disabuse him of this "your boy" notion.

"Really?" I said.

"I can hear 'em in there hunchin' it up!"

My heart began to race.

Hunchin'?

Perhaps it didn't quite mean what it seemed to mean.

I followed the child down the hall.

Rico had put aluminum foil on the walls and ceiling of the bathroom, spray painted half of it black.

Why? Lord knows!

A flap of this foil poked out from under the door by the child's knee, where he had bent down to get the best acoustics on the alleged "hunchin'."

I leaned down to where he was and put my ear to the door.

Hunchin'!

It was true and the noise, dear readers, was indescribable.

It staggered me.

I'm sure I went white as a ghost.

The child saw the confirmation in my eyes and a grin slowly spread across his face until it reached psychotic proportions.

"They in there hunchin'!" he yelled and began jerking the doorknob furiously.

Corn—who had outside the Boiler Room heard Rico ardently profess he would not have sex with Rachil until he was married, who had been up until this point seemingly vanquished in his quest for love—was in there hunchin' with Rachil!

My first love.

MFL!!!!!

How did this happen?

Where was Rico?

How had the triangle been violated so effortlessly, and without a scintilla of awareness on my part?

The child wanted to see.

I did not.

I felt faint.

I left the child pulling on the doorknob and walked out the big double doors at the front of the church into the yard, where I collapsed in a fever.

CHAPTER 7

I awoke in the shrubbery, mercifully undiscovered.

I saw the window of the church lit up and the three of them inside, laughing, as if reality were still intact.

Had I dreamed the hunchin'?

Was it simply one of my visions, which, already twenty-five years ago, had begun?

I had to know, and so here, at this time, I vowed to renew my observations in earnest as soon as I made it back to the dormitory to clean myself of the blood and vomit on my shirt.

I prayed my roommate would not be home, and, for once, my prayers were answered.

Thoroughly scrubbed with peppermint soap and a stiff washcloth, I breathed as best I could, and I plotted my course.

After a further week of observation, I reached a conclusion: that night I had indeed simply let my imagination run too free, for whatever "relationship" Corn and Rachil seemed to have secretly embarked upon, it was awkward and bumbling and, at first it seemed, free of penetration.

I noted many "inside" jokes and episodes of shrill, repressed laughter, but nothing more.

I admit, there was still cause for concern: Rico was noticeably more and more absent from the church, leaving Corn and Rachil alone.

Where was he?

At class?

At work?

No longer the sober Christian, he only appeared to sulk and drink at the church, then shuffle off to who knows where with his hippy friends, who were always stooped over some baggie of powder.

One night, Rachil cried to Corn about this distance and depression of Rico's, and there at the church, in the gluey yellow light, they kissed—I saw it, outraged—but then, rather than sprinting off to the bedroom to hunch, their amour disintegrated.

"We shouldn't," Rachil said.

"You're right," Corn said.

"What about Rico?" she said.

"Oh, yes. Rico," he said. "I worry about him so much."

(Liar!)

She embraced him, snuffling and leaking everywhere. I thought I could detect a sly grin on his face as he patted her shoulder a bit too much.

Regardless, it was clear that Rachil felt sorry for Rico and Corn, and Corn clearly thought this pity would be enough to allow him to work his dark magic on her.

I longed for him to try to play her one of his ballads, for surely that would allow her to see the sad bastard in his true light, but he had evidently accepted her pity as enough of a kind of love, one that earned him a victory over Rico, and so, a few nights later, he tried to kiss her ears, to put his hands on her little thighs.

She squirmed, sighed, equivocated, made fun of his prim clothes.

Drank.

Corn was thwarted!

But then, weeks later still, I came to the window late after an altercation at the bus station (not worth going into). I saw her pale thighs exposed in the living room, barely a shy mouthful for the lunging Corn mouth.

My mind made a fist.

"Wait," she said.

Withdrawn, his mouth dispossessed.

"Don't," she said, then giggled, pushing down her skirt. "Let's skip it and go to the Boiler Room."

I found I could breath again.

It was nothing.

Days passed.

The skirt stayed down.

But then I saw her again squirming away from his mouth, her hand covering her wet ear this time, and I wondered why these types of scenes kept happening—why didn't she simply call the police?

"Stop," she hissed.

He once more pushed his open mouth onto her taut lips anyway.

"Have you flossed?" she asked him.

Drooping back to the corner of the couch, he began to sulk.

"What?" she said. "It's disgusting! I don't want you slobbering all over my ears if you haven't flossed!"

(Good girl!)

"Fine," he said.

I know he hadn't flossed.

I know his belly was heavy with desire, his head leaden.

He tried to stroke her leg with a feigned casual finger from across the sofa, but she withdrew.

"I think you should go."

He rose to leave and I scrambled back to my spot in the scrub, delighted.

"I'll see you at the Boiler Room. Later," she said from the doorway.

"Fine," he said, moping across the driveway.

He had no power. They both knew it. We all knew it!

That night, rejected Corn went ahead to the bar (I followed), and there he started drinking with Rico, who no longer seemed concerned about winning Rachil's affection.

He spent quite a bit of time there at the bar, alone, his floral shirt gathering filth.

True, he had been in the hospital after complaining of auditory hallucinations to the student health center, and they sent him home to the church, where he cut his wrists with a kitchen knife.

Mesmerized, I watched the blood run over the white dinner plates he had set out on the table, but then I walked to a payphone and called the police so the plates wouldn't get too bloody before the firemen showed up.

I knew they would get sticky, so I let myself in to wash the plates as the ambulance pulled away from the church. I left no note, not needing acknowledgment of my good deed.

Rico had been prescribed a full menu of medications, including clonazepam, which he now handed over to Corn.

I sat there in the bar, in the booth behind the two "friends," taking mental notes and surreptitiously sipping gin from my thermos.

"As long as you don't plan on getting lucky tonight," Rico told Corn, his voice sluggish and detached, "you can take these and level out with no worries."

"No chance of getting lucky," Corn replied glumly, holding out his hand,"so, yes please."

"I thought you two . . . ?" Rico said, shaking the pills into Corn's palm.

"Nope. There's no chance," Corn said, though I noticed he had clearly flossed earlier. I saw the blood smeared on his incisors as he popped the pills into the back of his throat and washed them down with beer.

(Screenplay adaptation note: ROWDY MUSIC—BAR MONTAGE—THE CLASH—THE RAMONES—THE BAR PHONE RINGS—IT IS FOR CORN—A SMILE SPREADS ACROSS HIS FACE—FADE OUT)

CHAPTER 8

Corn sprinted out of the bar, nine blocks to Rachil's apartment.

I arrived later and saw from my tippy-toe perch—ghastly!—her hand gripping his forearm, pulling him into her room.

"You want this?" she whispered, or something to that effect. I couldn't quite hear as I settled atop the trash bins in the rear of the complex.

Why this sudden change? She didn't appear drunk. Mysterious.

Perhaps it was that they were now, instead of at the church, in *her* room, where the windows were more discreet. Perhaps she felt somehow "safe," away from a neighborly intrusion.

I noted that Corn was quite inebriated, the beer and the clonazepam working together to impede his fine motor skills while at the same time speeding up his speech.

He slushed his way through the conversation like some deranged snowshoer while his appendages twitched and dragged along independent of his mind.

It was true, of course, that Corn had been waiting a long time for this, so he had an absurd grin on his face that went beyond mere inebriation, but still managed to not quite be able to grasp the situation fully.

"How long is time?" he said, one arm shooting out spasmodically into the air. "Dunno, long enough that the duration isn't, like, a line, it's an arc, bent, pulling space in with it, long time, that's what I'm saying, a long time, I've wanted this a long time."

Things became quite stark for me then.

My breathing slowed and I felt a profound chill at the back of my skull.

Could she really be about to sleep with this silly, striving *child*?

Overcome by melancholy, I let my head droop; I could not watch.

But I knew my case required evidence, so I held my recorder up to the window and, despite the burning muscles in my shoulder, the tingling numbness in my forearms, I recorded the entire event.

Rather than relive it in the telling, I will simply here provide you with the transcript I've kept with me ever since.

1:28AM

(sounds of movement—furniture nudged, walls bumped)

Corn: "Wait, wait, wait! Why are we, you know, why are we doing it, like, now?"

Rachil: "Don't you want to?"

Corn: "Want to? *Want* to?"

(muffled sound of a body sliding headfirst across a bed-spread, dull thud)

Corn: (voice obscured by pillows) "I want to!"

(a zipper sounds, heels clatter, the wispy thumps of falling clothing)

Corn: "Special."

Rachil: "What?"

Corn: "Special . . . you're wearing . . . the special . . . the special . . ."

Rachil: "Oh my god, Corn. You are so *blitzed*."

Corn: "Undies!"

Rachil: (giggles) "You like?"

(sound of the bed creaking)

Corn: "I love. Looooooooooove looooooooooove the undies!"

(wet noises)

Rachil: "Wait. Wait. You'll be . . oh God this sounds so dumb, but you'll be gentle?"

Corn: "Oh yeah. Totally. Gentle Ben. Gentle Giant. Green Giant. Green Bean. Can a corn. You got it."

Rachil: "I'm nervous to try again. Last time was . . . weird."

Corn: "I flossed!"

(more wet noises, zippers, thumps)

Rachil: "What's wrong?"

Corn: "Huh?"

Rachil: "Don't you want to?"

Corn: "Rachil. C'mon. I've wanted to since, like, the brontosaurus wanted to with the lady brontosaurus, since the protozoa wanted to with the paramecium, since the big wanted to bang, since . . ."

Rachil: "Yeah but it just doesn't look like you're, you know, *ready*."

Corn: "What? I look totally ready! Got my shirt off, got my shoes off, or, one shoe off, anyway, got my pants off, got my . . . oh. Right."

(silence)

Corn: "True. I do not appear to be quite ready."

Rachil: (lower register) "Maybe I can help?"

Corn: "I don't know, I mean, unless you can give me a blood transfusion or have some Dippity-do or spackle or . . . oh, I see. The mouth. The job we call blow. Yes, by all means."

(horrible, horrible wet noises)

Rachil: "What the hell?"

(silence)

(bed creaks)

(sound of forehead being slapped)

Corn: "Oh . . . dear."

Rachil: "What?"

Corn: "Well, you see, I think . . . well, here's the thing. Thingy. Rico gave me some, uh, drugs."

Rachil: "Some what?"

Corn: "Drugs. Clonazepam. I think it's called clonazepam. It's a painkiller. I think. Or relaxer. Something. It's not good for the . . . the sex. But it's great for the mood. Moooooood."

Rachil: (laughs)

(silence)

Rachil: (cries)

Corn: (unintelligible whispers)

Rachil: (sobs)

(zippers)

Corn: "Where are you going?"

Rachil: "The couch. I hope you can continue to enjoy yourself, but this is . . . it's just not . . . it's not good, Corn."

(sobs)

(door closes)

Corn: "Rachil!"

(silence)

Corn: "Rachil?"

Corn: "This bed is . . . soft."

(snoring)

(crickets)

CHAPTER 9

The night was hot, but vigilance requires sacrifice.

Corn woke up, ready, but Rachil had gone to sleep on the couch, alone.

I remember the piney thickness of the air hung on me.

I had watched the sun mush across the horizon where loose formations of heat-drunk birds sliced the air.

She had feigned sleep when he returned to her. She kept her eyes and jaw closed, said, "You should go."

He didn't.

She opened her eyes.

"Go," she said through gritted teeth.

I thought it was finally over for him, that I could finally swoop in and sweep Rachil off her feet with true chivalry.

I spent the day scrounging at the dining hall, eating discarded oranges and sardines in the kitchen until that evening, when I settled into my station outside Rachil's apartment with renewed gusto, awaiting Corn's final humiliation.

Surely she would see after the previous night's fiasco that neither Corn nor Rico were the one she wanted—right?

I would be there to see it all fall apart . . . or so I thought!

I found, to my dismay, that Rachil had, in a kind of fit, rearranged the furniture in her room so I could now barely see around a bookshelf positioned directly in front of the window.

My spirits became damp.

Worse, Corn returned apparently sober, contrite, mewling apologies and encomiums.

I threw my packet of salt peanuts to the ground in disgust and once again set up my recording device. It would turn out to be one of the more horrifying experiences of my young life.

From what I could later decipher from the recording—in the moment it was an indecipherable hell—Corn managed to consummate his attack thusly: after a final tearful apology, she went to him, bleary with tears, to kiss him hard on the mouth.

There was blood.

Then: him, silent; her, a throaty coaxing; then, tears; then, a fat slapping of broad back skin; then, her, pleading with him, in her confusion, NOT to stop; then, yes; then, yes; then, yes . . . again, again, again they had wild, passionate, joyous intercourse on the floor of her apartment.

After half an hour, I found I could not watch, merely held my recorder at the window.

I find that I return to the recording to listen more often than I would have first thought, and I have recently had it digitized through a service so I can listen on my portable mp3 player.

"What do you want, baby?" she coos, probably wiping tears away, at the 15:23 mark.

He dutifully keeps at it, saying nothing as the floor creaks mightily for a full two minutes.

"Talk to me, baby, tell me what you want," she moans through her teeth at 17:54.

He must have thought that if he spoke she would start crying again, so he let her lie there with her head most likely turned toward the side, asking no one her questions while he pumped in a fever.

The entire recording lasts twenty-seven minutes, twelve seconds.

The last minute is a sickly silence punctuated only by labored breathing.

The last thing said: "Maybe we should get a drink."

They quickly dressed and set off for the bar while I sat in silent hell.

What saddens me most, dear readers, is that Corn didn't seem to even *want to* have sex with her throughout the entire experience!

He was not like the rest of us.

He clearly just didn't want her to have sex with anyone else—not Rico, not me, not anyone—so he humped and hunched, made his noises, attempting to send his vector slicing through everything.

I sometimes listen to the recording while watching *Joan of Arc,* sketching winter trees in my notebook.

I'm not a victim.

I know it may look as if I am in these circumstances, and I am no doubt the aggrieved party here, but a lifetime of such challenges has shown that I am far from a victim, that I am a survivor, that my resilience outshines any pitiful aggressions put forth in opposition!

Does this negligible moderator think he can outlast me?

Does he think I will simply go away?

He is mistaken.

As Sun Tzu says in the *Art of War,* "He who cares more, wins."

I win.

I had a choice in my life as to whether or not I would become a victim, and I won't lie: it was tempting.

As a bright-eyed innocent I had no idea what cruelties this life had in store for me, and so I thought that I could join the crowd, that my sensitivities and perceptions were not so abnormal as to exclude me from the activities of the group.

But "the group" has brought us to this lowly point in our history.

Did Brecht dance with Hitler?

No.

Nor shall I.

This feeling I have tonight is not good.

It's as if my whole being, from my sinuses to my soul, has been stuffed with wet wool smelling of cat's breath.

But then, every so often—and who can predict when?—a bolt crackles through me, a painful lucidity during which all my grievances synchronize to emit light and sound, animation, which I record, the life of the mind—captured!—and I convey it to you.

Remarkable, yes, but I fear what I'm capable of in these moments.

The group knows not what it is excluding.

Perhaps, though, Chris does indeed know what it's like to be excluded, for he looks upon the only slightly older generation and sees what he will never be able to live up to.

Rather than take the true measure of his inadequacy and accept his place, he derides and dismisses.

How I wish I could explain to Rachil and Charli that I have, in fact, learned from this formative experience!

I now know that to be a mere spectator, as I was in the dry-humping instance, is not the way to truly embody point X, that I must use what skills I have to go beyond mere observation into the realm of action.

Though don't mistake me: language deployed is an action!

Language deployed affects the world, performs alchemy, my dears, yes, and I believe my words, my private "spells" and visions, have had some effect on reality, though back then, at the window, I confess I didn't behave as I should have.

I kept silent.

While that vile reed of a boy stole my Rachil's innocence I should have yelled out, or burst in and split his head open with a tree branch—I did have one handy—but I did nothing.

I froze.

My condition overcame me.

The sounds—the gymnastic grunts and muffled tussles in that apartment—mesmerized me, and my world fell away.

Though I did learn a valuable lesson: I am not a regular man.

I cannot simply swing my fists to get what I want!

I must use my mind, my linguistic gift, my talent for revelation.

True, it did seem then as if my passivity enabled Corn to "win" the girl while Rico wilted, and so it seemed I had failed.

I certainly thought I had at that time.

But I persisted and lo, my actions enabled the girl at least a glimpse of life outside the confines of sexual slavery!

Was it a waste of time?

To let Corn push his fat tongue into my girl's mouth in some decrepit apartment complex that summer?

What did she get?

Not "closure" with Rico, which is what she had surely hoped for.

You see, Rachil was like me.

She liked to think systematically.

She had work to do, a list to get through, and she would've had a hard time with it if she'd had Rico on her mind all the time.

I realized then that what Corn wanted wasn't her, and that was why she had no problem giving "it" up to him.

He had developed a role for her in his story, but it wasn't, she knew, her true role in her own life—she would not give herself to him in any real way, but she was a charitable person, a kind person, and also, she thought, a person who solved problems.

And Corn had a problem.

Many, actually, but her place in his life, in Rico's life, made up a powerful knot of problems she could undo by giving up twenty minutes, by not thinking about Corn's wretched flossing habits, about how he said he liked to let it "all build up" before getting in there with the floss.

She would kiss him.

She, who flossed every day and sometimes every night too, would kiss his nasty mouth if it would solve his problems.

She kissed him again and again and let his dull weight push down on her.

In these moments, he reminded me of a little dog humping a leg, staring with those doggy eyes, thrusting. "Give it! Give it! Give it!"

Fine, she seemed to say, take what you think will help you.

CHAPTER 10

After a few weeks, it was better than it had been at first, for I could no longer hear what I conceived to be crying.

The feeling that had seemed to overtake Rachil in the middle of the doggy moment, Corn's eyes surely imploring her to "give it," his breath pouring down on her until she'd be forced to gulp down a sob, then another, until she found herself turning her head away and crying into her pillow.

That feeling seemed to have melted away, because, she must have realized, this was not her life.

Her life was elsewhere, in the realm of pure forms, as mine was.

Surely what she really wanted was for Corn not to simply stop (as she strangely still pleaded with him NOT to do), but to disappear completely, to disintegrate into the ether, and for morning to arrive—coffee, toast, what to wear, and no question of his blubbering neediness until later that night.

That had to be the reason he was never allowed to sleep over.

The sharp angles of the morning belonged to her alone.

She and I, for a time, running parallel in the morning light.

CHAPTER 11

We ran parallel for a time, but after a few months I couldn't bear to watch or listen any longer.

I began spending more and more time wandering about the campus, conversing with my bereft self about various world events.

I found myself returning again and again to thoughts of Rico and the nervous system—had I made a mistake somewhere?

I'm sure you're wondering, dear readers: why did I take such a liking to Rico?

Why did I so prefer this bonehead to the other?

A feeling, friends. I went on a gut feeling.

Also, of course, I had studied T. E. Lawrence, and so I knew where I needed to attack if I had any hopes of winning.

Corn was clearly the head of the operation, Rachil the heart, and poor, sensitive Rico the nervous system.

I would have no luck with direct action against the head or heart, but I had just the resources and resolve to attack the nervous system.

Guerilla warfare, my dears!

I knew he was fragile, but I didn't quite know how fragile, how confused, how on the precipice of total collapse he was.

True, he had seemed ungainly and unstable, not only in matters of dress—he had at this point taken to making his own brand of bewildering T-shirts with nonsensical slogans and illustrations on them—but in temperament as well.

He may have simply still been suffering from the effects of his auditory hallucinations. I'm not sure.

He also could have been exhausted from overwork, for while Corn had landed a cherry projection-booth gig as some kind of nefarious quid pro quo with the university's technical services department, Rico had been forced to labor outside the confines of the academy, at the "Parkside Loco" Bar and Grill, AND for the city's recreation services department.

It was in this latter capacity that fate once again threw us together.

CHAPTER 12

After a long night of rambles, I arrived at the North Campus sports complex to watch, as had become my new custom, the intramural girls' soccer game.

I loved seeing these vigorous young women exerting themselves confidently in their Umbro shorts, underwear at times visible via binoculars, stocky legs flexing in kneesocks . . . the perfect end to a long night of chaste reflection!

I had just been packing up my cooler when I caught sight of a familiar slouch at the southwest corner of the field.

I recognized that mix of rigid posture, hunched shoulders, and doughy gut making its way onto the field, the new game's "referee" in his regulation blue polo shirt half-tucked into his khaki shorts.

His disproportionately skinny ankles were stuck in a pair of scuffed boat shoes and his walk had that flapping quality, a jalopy rhythm that was unmistakably Rico's.

Perhaps, I thought to myself, this totally unexpected reunion was an indication from Beyond that I should not leave off my study of Corn and Rachil and Rico quite yet, that the fates were telling me that all was not lost, that the nervous system could use a jolt!

I unpacked my thermos once again as the girls cleared off, a few looking nervously over their shoulders at bumbling Rico as he did a few perfunctory and useless stretches.

As these taut and tight ladies cleared the field of play, a ragged crew of balding men appeared, stretching and slapping backs, affixing flag belts to their blown-out waists.

After an interval of greeting and lining up, Rico blew his whistle and the game—a flag football affair between older faculty men—began.

The men, divided by makeshift blue and gray uniforms, played with unsightly vigor, but amidst this terrible play, Rico dodged and waved, expertly facilitating the game, so that as these aged gents maneuvered, I found myself applauding!

I—a young man who couldn't care less about such "sports"—became, because of Rico's maestro-like management of the affair, particularly invested in the outcome of this game, in the victory of the blue shirts.

Why did I cheer for blue?

Again, readers: a feeling.

I began taking bets with the other spectators—a ragged few—there on the risers, and my voice grew hoarse with cheering for my Blues.

Dear readers, I should tell you here that I have a history with games of chance.

The upward narrative arc of my childhood took a precipitous dive when my mother became engulfed in gaming.

A casino is a theme park where the theme is money.

At first, I loved outings to both the casino and the track, even when I stayed in the parking lot with my Sony Watchman for most of the afternoon.

I loved them because I knew eventually my mother would come out for advice, and I would tell her what dogs and what horses to put money on, what combinations to leverage.

Until I hit puberty and my brain developed the wrinkle that processes disappointment and time, gambling with Mother was my favorite thing.

But, I saw after an interval, she had no system.

She'd bet a hundred dollars on the dog who peed before the race, the horse with the best coloring, the slot machine with Elvis on it—whatever spoke to her at the last second.

She had a muse similar to mine, a gut with similar feelings, except every time these bets and these long afternoons of gambling turned bust (which they inevitably did), it became further proof for her that she had been cosmically wronged.

She deserved an easy life, nice clothes, a fancy car, a paid-for house—she *deserved* these things, and yet they were not hers.

Looking back, I don't know why she believed in the good life, but every time the pee-dog floundered, the pretty horse threw its jockey, or Elvis stared out at her with the stone-cold face of the Buddha, she fell apart.

And when you see the stone-cold face of the Elvis Buddha making your mother cry, you yourself *naturally* fall apart a little too.

Not anymore.

I do not fall apart, because I see she throws good money after bad, that she concentrates too much on suckers' games, and because she does all of it without a system.

Since I've had a few wiry hairs "down there," her lack of system has driven me bananas.

At fourteen, I could stride confidently past the entrance security to sit in the stands.

I'd ask her to place a quinella on a raft of carefully selected breeders' delights culled from the finest gambling periodicals available at the peanut stand, and then I would sit with my program rolled tight, hollering rapid-fire encouragement to my horses at the top of my still-awkward lungs.

Mother's little gambler won more than a few.

But it was never enough to outpace Mother's losses, so no one ever went home happy until I came "of age" and could play the ultimate game—blackjack.

Of course, Mother never figured out if she liked it when I really started winning—for, you see, my muse was a winner, and when I won, when I slid my chips into the circle and watched a woman named Mona with skin the color of an overcooked hot dog flip my cards, every cell in my body would synchronize and emit a cherry-red light, because this was how it was supposed to be—more money for us!

But I lost too, of course, and in losing my money I would also lose control of my mind.

My system would break down, or worse, I would not have been disciplined enough to stick with the system and so . . .

The injustice of it, how money meant for me had gone to some Serbian in leather pants, made me—I admit—feel bitter, and even more entitled, caused me to spew waspish comments at anyone and everyone, just like, I see now, Mother.

The betting circle on the felt was like a pie in the face.

The flop of the cards on the table was a box of my ears.

It was not right.

Someone, I thought then, should pay.

If anyone had cared enough to see how angry I became while gambling, they might have told me the only one really suffering for my sins was me, but mostly everyone just steered clear if I'd been out gambling, including, especially after the last divorce, Mother.

"Isn't the whole thing that the house always wins?" you ask.

"Not if you have a system," I reply. "Not at blackjack."

Do I remember when the toothless pamphleteer told me that Christ could help ease my bitterness and my sense of entitlement and my gambling problem?

Yes.

I told him to "get lost," but on nights when I played my bad hands over and over in my mind until I couldn't stop seeing the king of diamonds flipping on top of my seven and five of hearts, my stack of chips pulled away by Mona's hot dog hands, I did think to call on a Christian oblivion to stop my mind from unspooling.

The Lord is my shepherd. I shall not want.

I tried it.

Repeated it in my mind over and over to crowd out the cards, but the problem was I did want.

I wanted more money.

I deserved it.

Next time.

Oh yes, all of those gambling nights came back to me as I sat there on the bleachers watching the flag-football game.

Things did become a bit blurry for me as the game wore on—I reached for my thermos of vodka and found it was strangely empty—but I did gather through the fog that it had been a closely fought but rather unremarkable display up until "the moment."

With time running out and the gray shirts down only three points, thirty yards from the end zone, there came the "hike."

A scrum.

I watched the arc of a wobbly pass as it fell through the mist into the arms of a man in a gray T-shirt who had huffed and puffed into the end zone.

A catch!

The huff-and-puff lump looked around, astonished at his good fortune in securing the "pigskin," and then, because he had achieved something no mere spectator could have (I admit it), he danced.

He pointed his little fingers up and down, and he involved his android pelvis in the dance.

To my right on the risers, the knot of gray shirt partisans erupted in high fives at the sight of this score.

"No!" I yelled, leaning over to swat the fives away from completion, disgusted. *Injustice!*

The other spectators, my compatriots, slumped and frowned along with me.

One patted me on the back and murmured wet reassurances into my ear.

Crumpled bills and cigarettes exchanged hands as we all began to "settle up"—I saw red all around me—but, oh ho, what was this?

Shouts from the field stopped us short.

Rico—lovely, justice-serving Rico!—was shaking his head and signaling a dead play, defiantly crossing his arms in front of his chest.

"No way, sirs!" he yelled. "The QB was down!"

He pointed back to where the QB stood sheepishly, hands on his hips, a flag forlorn on the grass beside him.

The gray partisans above and below cried out in protest, but rules are rules, so the players jogged back down the field to huddle up again.

I felt suddenly refreshed.

Sober.

"There are *rules!*" I screamed. "There is *justice!* When the QB is down, there are *consequences!* And Rico knows this! He recognizes! Mother, take heed!"

The game was over; the Blues won.

I don't remember exactly what happened next. I was so overjoyed that my mind raced in a fever as grumbling gentlemen in ponchos and army jackets stuffed my hands with money. I began then and there to truly admire and feel such an affinity for Rico.

My "gut" was inspired!

I tried to suppress a belch by ducking my chin and flexing my abs, but a dark rattle shot through my nasal passages and made my eyes sting.

Always partial to the game of Risk (my system: always take Kamchatka early), I saw the latest gambling scene on the quad as a negative image of a real war, with the old and "infirm" risking it all at the front, on the "ball field" in their blue and gray, battling for favor and pride, gentlemen of a certain age with bad mortgages, broken marriages, and kids who despise them, all dotting the fields playing these "games" to determine which group is the better (UNION VS. CONFEDERACY?), while the youths of the world looked on.

He enacted justice.

This, I thought, was a young man of the future!

A compatriot!

If I am not able to have Rachil, then by God, Rico should!

Elated, I followed him from the field onto the city bus (late, as always), and I observed him closely as he sank into his seat in contemplation.

I assumed, perhaps, he was thinking of how to solve the war—the one outside the city limits, the state, the county, the region, the USA, the continent—to seal it in time and give it over to reenactors and historians.

That is what I had been contemplating there on the bus, so I said aloud to all the passengers, "Develop an alternative energy strategy and let the indigenous sort themselves out. Simple!"

I believe Rico would have agreed with me, but I saw too late that he had a worn paperback in his hands and a nefarious set of headphones on his head.

If only he had turned back to talk to me then we might have come together to solve a foreign policy struggle that still plagues us as a country to this day, but he did not ask for my ideas on the subject. No one, in fact, had asked for my ideas on the subject, just my *tact* in not mentioning it to anyone—especially not on the bus!

But of course I have always refused tact!

I have, in fact, long advocated for the war.

Everyone I know has been horrified at my advocacy (I should share with you some of THOSE arguments, my dears!), but to Rico, I see now, my advocacy surely would have made sense. (He would now, I'm sure, understand my position on the blog; one cannot be neutral in the conflict between freedom and oppression.)

He would see that I refuse to give tacit approval to oppression, that I have fought against it in whatever capacity I could throughout my life.

Rico would know instinctively that I clamor for a fight, a new narrative, a patriotism of the left that won't disdain the soldiers who protect it.

Later, while his City Parks basketball team practiced lay-ups in the gym, I sat in the bleachers reading aloud from Thomas Paine, did I not?

And when I drew up plays for the team as an extra help to the coach, I consulted this new "counterinsurgency" strategy, yes?

A glorious time!

I had felt once again like I was part of a country! And a team!

I could have been, if not great, then quite good at basketball, dear readers, so this is not just idle claptrap.

Up until ninth grade I was considered one of the top players in my class, an avid defender, an annoyance deployed by the coaches to harass the opponent's best scorer.

But my weakness, where I so desperately needed tutelage, was with my jump shot.

Oh sure, occasionally I would "stroke it" and hit numerous shots in a row during practice, such that my teammates would marvel at my ability and give me little pats on the behind.

But in games something happened. Some mania would overtake me.

Perhaps it was that I wanted my form to be perfect.

I'm not sure.

But I would catch a pass and—wide open!—square to shoot.

I would repeat the mantra I had made for myself: "Knees, elbow, wrist!"—shorthand for "bend at the knees; lock the elbow in; follow through with the wrist; *make the shot.*" but the game happened so quickly that I would catch the pass and chant my chant in a rush only to find my body could not keep up with my mind. (Or, maybe, that my mind could not keep up with my body?)

Nothing would behave.

My knees would dip too low, my elbow would creep out too wide, and my wrist would lock into place so the barely spinning orb would be sent into the ether, never to hit the backboard/rim apparatus.

Naturally I became an object of ridicule amongst my "peers," and instead of taking me under his wing to tutor me in technique and strategy—I would have been such a pupil!—the incompetent hack of a coach *cut me* from the squad!

Crushed, I renounced the game.

For years I refused to even acknowledge a pair of sneakers on television.

They were dead to me.

Over time, yes, I came back to the game, but by then my prime had passed, my skills had atrophied, and my talent had gone fallow, all thanks to an ignoramus coach!

I have resolved not to let the same thing happen to the kids in my current location, who practice at the recreation center, but has anyone thanked me?

No!

In fact, they have had on numerous occasions the janitorial staff escort me from the facility!

Rico clearly felt bad about all of this.

I watched him let out a deep sigh a few nights later at the "Parkside Loco," no doubt upset with himself he hadn't been more understanding about my "coaching" at the gym.

Shame tickled the back of his throat.

He made it to the shrimp "buffet" with his cleaning rag, but there he quite naturally gagged.

Flies buzzed.

I snuck over to him and whispered from behind my napkin as he adjusted the plates and forks:

"Did you know that Sartre said he never had a day of despair in his entire life?"

Rico made no indication that he heard me, though I said it repeatedly.

Flummoxed, I began chewing on my napkin, but then I saw that Rico must have indeed heard me, for he suddenly slipped away from the puce shrimp and walked downstairs shaking his head.

Parts of the restaurant were under construction, and a drop cloth and a can of paint had been shoved behind the creaky bathroom door just to the left of the stairs.

The smell of glue and sawdust swirled into my nostrils as I snuck to the door just as Rico closed it.

A draft wafted in from behind me as Rico undid his "Button Fly" shorts to urinate, but before he could unfurl a stream into the bowl, he tensed.

Looking back over his shoulder, directly at what had become my regular "observation crack" in the door, Rico suddenly stepped back with an impish grin on his face, causing me to inhale sharply and feel my heartbeat in my throat.

Had I been caught?

He took two steps to the corner, and—rather than press his face into the crack to confront me with his crazy eyes—he bent over to the paint can and stirring stick.

He popped open the paint can with his keys, then reached for his dangling genitalia.

Strange.

Was it part of his job?

Was he required to finish painting?

No.

Dear readers, he dipped the tip of his penis into the can of taupe paint.

It must have felt quite cool there on his (uncircumcised) penis, because he smiled a rather too large smile as he dunked his member in the paint like a "Long John" into coffee.

Then, waddling over to the sink—can in hand, penis in can—Rico smiled his crack-toothed smile ever wider and let out a hiccoughy giggle.

Giddiness began to course through my own crouched arteries as well.

What a marvel was this Rico!

The nervous system, indeed!

What would he do next?

With his left knee propped up on the sink and his right hand guiding his dripping, taupe penis, he spelled out, awkwardly (and, it appeared, a bit painfully), a word on the bathroom mirror.

At first I couldn't make it out, for his hunched frame blocked my view, but at last, after he gave a satisfied grunt and slid back from the sink, I saw it—I knew he still carried the torch!—all was not lost!—"R-A-C-H-I-L-!"

The last of the *!* dripped down into the sink.

(Despair! Never in his life!)

The paint must have begun to sting his penis hole, because Rico had no time to admire his work before he began hopping back and forth on the balls of his feet.

He ran the hot water into his cupped hand while whispering a series of hushed "ow"-like utterances.

FYI: Having just performed this same paint-by-penis procedure in the name of research here in the bathroom I share with the filthy rabble on my floor, I surmise it took a bit more than just warm water to remove *all* of the paint from Rico's penis.

Rico scrubbed a little with his thumb, then commenced his delayed urination in the general direction of the bowl.

(Urination causes quite a few more "ow"s.)

I watched a single drop of urine fall on his left shoe and, there in my observational crouch, shook my head in wonder at Rico's fashion sense—those shoes!

Once again, boat shoes with no socks!

The boy suffered for fashion.

It was summer, so he had hundreds of little bites on the tops of his feet and on his bare ankles.

Mosquitoes must have loved to feast on his fragrant blood.

Even here in my room, I scratch at the red nubs covering my own ankles, having similar blood, though I mitigate the blood feast with daily doses of garlic from my own private stock I plant every year in an abandoned lot near my residence.

My favorite variety is a Spanish garlic I have dubbed "Don Legarto."

I pop five to six cloves of Don Legarto in my mouth a day, and yet still the mosquitoes feast, infernal creatures!

The tight shoes rubbed, but Rico knew pain was not so different in quality from pleasure, and besides, he had developed a strong mind and so chose to ignore the waves of red pricklings washing up his shins.

Or, rather, to savor them.

As I do now.

He left the bathroom and his (loud and clear!) message behind.

He wiped a tear from his right eye.

As a teenager, Rico partially blinded himself in this right eye when he tried to juggle three five-pound weights in a rank weight room used by his high school track team.

I imagine Rico must have thought juggling was a state of mind, and so he saw no need to practice, a theory he no doubt picked up from his idiot buddy Corn.

In actual practice, of course, one weight ricocheted off the other, which hit the next, and that one clanked onto the upper left quadrant of Rico's face.

It's only hubris if you fail.

His best friend had surely said that, just as my own step-father did, lording over my hospital bed with his dark mane and his craggy face when I finally came to after one of my own high school accidents.

"What accidents?" you ask?

I know I seem so free of trouble, how could there have possibly been accidents?

There were many: Fall from roof, boiling water spill, errant BB puncture, thigh stab (pencil), thigh stab (stick), curbside tooth crack, and, of course, football leg.

Football!

Why didn't I think of this earlier?

As I watched Rico's game, it must have been this trauma that made me feel so strongly that sense of justice finally being served.

Oh, the memory stings worse than paint in a penis hole!

Back then, I merely wanted to play with my peers like any other boy.

I would have never called them "friends," for I had no one I could call what Montaigne called "fast friends" besides the loathsome Daniel and Emmett.

Beyond these two, I merely had a crowd of airheaded contemporaries I was forced to spend my high school days with in torpor and resignation. I signed up for football thinking perhaps it promised a kind of excitement.

Oh yes, now it seems comical.

Shouldn't I have known better?

Well, yes, of course, I should have, but at fourteen?

Surely we can't expect boys of fourteen to accept the horrid world as it is without any hope for change? Whatever your opinion on the subject, the fact of the case is that I joined the freshman football squad.

It was even more of a disaster than you can imagine, even before the fateful incident that permanently affected my development.

Merciless taunts, a total lack of compassion, willful misguidance, practical jokes, all at my expense.

And then, just as I resolved to leave the field of play forever, I was called in to play running back for one play in an obscene practice.

I know I should have refused and flung my helmet into the crow-infested trees.

What would they have done?

What could they possibly have done to me that would have been worse than what actually happened?

Nothing.

Of course—nothing.

But I gleefully took up the gauntlet as my sniveling peer group chortled on the sidelines.

I strapped the cursed helmet on—filthy thing stinking of plasticky sweat—and jogged out to the huddle.

I confess, I imagined some small moment of glory, a fraction of what the other boys received daily, if only just to understand something more about the carefree psychic terrain they romped through.

The play was called and lo, I was to receive the ball in a handoff and run behind hulking number 44, Clint Nester, fullback *extraordinaire*!

The huddle clapped in unison—my last gesture of group solidarity, I swear it now if I did not then—and lined up in position.

The cliché rings true.

It all happened so fast.

The center snapped the ball, the quarterback shoved it in my gut with a sneer.

I followed number 44 through what appeared to be an opening in the defensive line, but then—nothing.

A minute later, I came to.

I was flat on my back with horrible stinking weight crushing down on my leg, darkness, and a blinding pierce shooting up my appendage.

I was trapped.

I heard laughter outside the wet-sock heat of the pile, but all I could see were the grimy jerseys and pads writhing above me, and then Clint Nester—my own teammate!—lurched into view with an insane leer smeared across his face.

Our masks separated us, but I could taste his sour soda breath twisting around my uvula.

Panic began to rise, even before I felt his grubby paw push my facemask up while another boy—hand slithering from God knows where—pressed his thumb under my jawbone, into the soft part of my chin (a "pressure point," I later found out).

The panic swirled in my core.

They grunted out their laughter as the pile continued to squirm all around me, and then—I can barely admit it even now, thirty years on—Clint Nester, oppressor, performed a heinous act.

He pushed his own facemask up, stretched out his neck, and he licked me!

His slabby damp tongue ran along my Adam's apple, worse than a blade.

I went blind with rage, released sounds inhuman and unfamiliar to nature.

Of course I thought I had friends on the team, a few other outcast boys who sympathized with my plight as I did with theirs.

We had made a pact, a tacit one, but a pact nonetheless, that if any of us were singled out unnecessarily by the popular, the adept, the regular boys, why, we'd stand with the injured party!

But of course as soon as I heard that god-awful snapping and felt that insanity-producing tongue, I turned to those boys—my friends!—and I saw them through the maze of cleats and ankles snickering with the rest on the sidelines, basking in the transitory approval of the mob.

It affected me much more than the pain in my leg (a pain I still suffer from, not incidentally).

Having my friends, my comrades, turn on me when I needed them most, it plunged me into a deep depression.

I had loved my fellows as much—if not more—than myself, but lying there in agony in the lawn clippings and litter, I felt my ultimate solitude engulf me in an instant.

I would be alone from then on.

Or I should say, since I had been alone up until then as well but was innocent of it, I knew I would be alone from then on and this knowledge had the potential to retard my development irreversibly.

And my leg was broken underneath it all.

CHAPTER 13

Pain.

Freud.

That perverted psychopath made it a cliché to say that sex is violent, but it is nonetheless true, and Rico knew then—just as I had since the Football Tongue Imbroglio—that this particular truth contained a still more radical truth within it: love itself is violent.

How can one person trust another if he (or she!) knows that the other has the capacity to love?

Would you, dear readers, stake your life on the supposition that the love might be directed at you, only you, forever and ever?

No!

You would not!

You're not insane!

So we can imagine now that Rico, being a somewhat bright and sensitive young man, was suspecting he would not, knowing that Rachil did indeed have the capacity to love, stake his own life on the supposition that she would somehow use this capacity to love *him*.

There at the Parkside Loco, ignoring the painful bites on his ankles and the sting in his penis hole and the tears in his eyes, he came to a conclusion: love *itself* was violent.

He was not.

He had learned this after he failed to take up arms against his friend when the sneaky rapist—and why not call him by that name?—stole Rico's love away from him there at the church.

And so being nonviolent, perhaps it followed that Rico himself did not actually love?

Not in the way Rachil did, evidently.

He might, in the end, not have the capacity to love.

There, beside the shrimp buffet, under the twirling fans, he looked as if he thought he might feel this lack of capacity acutely, that it might portend some awful, lonely end to his life.

I could tell he had become fearful of the pain love caused.

Rachil was dangerous.

His feelings for Rachil even more so.

Love was dangerous.

So he was, because of Corn, reconsidering his life.

This is sad, dear readers, yes, but all was not lost.

A young woman strode by in a knit cotton dress that had been hastily pulled over a bathing suit; Rico and I both noticed the damp bikini's outline.

This bikini held (loosely) a firm pair of buttocks.

I gave out a yip, a signal to Rico to let nature take its course, to allow himself to begin to think of other women, for other women would surely make Rachil jealous and draw her back to him.

Rico was not as unfamiliar with other young women as I then thought, I found out later when so many flocked to his defense.

Each of Rico's previous girlfriends—three from high school and two from his first year at college—when asked what she saw in him, mentioned, if you can believe it, the allure of his always slightly milky and always slightly out of focus right eye.

Many other women who have not ended up girlfriends of Rico surely find it repulsive.

There is a little dark coloring in the iris and there is copious, unsentimental weeping from the corners.

But Rico had realized something that took me decades to learn: there is no use trying to please everyone.

In fact, the idea of individual taste can be used to one's advantage.

A girl who wants to think of herself as an individual can be flattered into thinking she is via a deranged eyeball, or, in my case, a veritable cornucopia of physical oddities.

Who knew?

Rico!

Bravo, Rico!

If he did not love, Rico would, he most likely reasoned at this point, rather not be lonely.

The young woman in the wet bikini swanned into her seat, her smooth legs crossing like clouds.

The other fish in the sea swam up into Rico's (and my) vision.

Ladies.

Gents.

We can now imagine Rico began here considering these other possibilities truly just as soon as the last drip of taupe paint dripped into the sink in the bathroom down below.

You see—I've only just now made this connection—language *is* action!

Rico expelled a demon from within his soul by deploying the totem word in taupe paint with his penis on the mirror there at the Parkside Loco.

These things work, dear readers, though I don't fault you your skepticism.

Rico was entering a new phase, a secret time I'm sure even now Rachil knows little about, since she was off cavorting with the evil other, Corn, at the time of this transformation.

I'm confident you've experienced something akin to a certain feeling Rico felt during this secret time, and so you are well aware that there comes a time when the person you thought you were dies.

A time when you behave in such a way that has no relation to your conception of who you are.

"I would not do this," you think, "I am not this kind of person," and yet you *are* doing it, so the only conclusion is that you are not the person you thought you were.

This can be quite crushing.

It's called in various circles "becoming an adult" and/or "growing up" and/or "having a psychotic episode."

I admit I held this particular crisis at bay for longer than anyone could have reasonably expected, which may have been the reason it was so traumatic when it did arrive for me.

I'm not sure.

When I was old enough to know better, years after the Football Incident and the Parissa Disaster, I found myself still hanging around with this couple of fellow outcasts, Daniel and Emmett.

I mistakenly thought that my status as an outsider, as a reject from the wretched society of young yes-men and frigid debutantes, signaled some flaw in me, so I took up with whomever I could, an error I've made only rarely in the years hence.

These lonely hooligans—Emmett with his pathetic downy mustache and Daniel with his bog-like complexion—would lounge about Daniel's mother's home on afternoons while our peers were performing their after-school athletic feats and self-servicing "civic" duties.

This dank duo had other plans.

They would concoct various schemes to amuse and challenge themselves while laying about Daniel's den, then, as the sun went down, set out to spread their filth.

How so?

One example: they would rummage through the trash of the town's one illicit newsstand in hopes of finding discarded scraps of titillating images—a half breast here, a pudenda there—and then they would shove these scraps into the mail slots of priggish girls' homes.

Also: they would order furniture C.O.D. to the science teacher's house, stretch plastic wrap across a busy intersection or two to see what kind of chaos they could stir up, make prank phone calls to grunt obscene noises at elderly women.

That kind of thing.

These two had regaled me some history-class afternoon with tales of their derring-do, and I suppose I tried to impress them with an offering of my own.

"That's nothing," I said, idly sharpening a pencil with my pocketknife. "If you really want to do something fun . . ."

And then I told them of an idea I had nurtured since a late-night drive from my Meema's home when I was a five-year-old.

The idea was this:

To cut a piece of cardboard into a rough approximation of a midsized mammal—a raccoon, a cat, a dog, or opossum.

Then, paint this approximation black on both sides.

Cut four almond-shaped eyes from a sheet of aluminum foil and affix these—two to a side—to the creature's head.

Create some kind of stand for the creature so it will rest on its own, upright.

Then, after the sun has gone down, place this creature in the middle of a road, preferably a winding, dark road with a moderate amount of traffic—not so much, of course, that you would be spotted putting it out, but enough that you wouldn't have to wait hours for a "victim."

Finally, wait in the nearby bushes for the aluminum eyes to reflect the headlights of an oncoming vehicle.

The driver will have to then decide if he (or she) is prepared to take a life for his (or her) ease of transportation.

Genius!

Needless to say, Emmett and Daniel nearly burst at the seams in fits of spittley cackles at the plot.

I was once again accepted, though I admit I felt a tickle of shame in my seated region.

Why did I try to impress these buffoons?

Regardless, I was breathless for the bell, and, as soon as it rang, we sprinted to Daniel's house.

Drunk on their acceptance, I tried to smile through the rest of the afternoon.

The den smelled of cabbage and crock-pot, feet and some peculiar boy rankness that I had only mild whiffs of at home.

Daniel's older brother Frank lay half-dead in an armchair, shirt off, conspicuous hairs.

He seemed partially disabled, slumped behind us, watching TV with a dead face.

He sent a chill through my being.

I often think of him now as a kind of cautionary tale when I find myself descending into sloth, idly clicking through photos of young women.

When night fell—early in a country January: 4:45PM—we set out through the snow with our "cat."

With no little difficulty, we established our craft in the center of the road, just before a patch of ice, and then we scurried into the ditch.

I watched the clouds of our breath expanding out into the night air at intervals.

No one spoke.

We tensed as one when we heard the high idle of some town car making its way up the hill, when, out of the darkness, its headlights crested the hill.

No breath.

Need I go on?

Must you torture me with this memory, you infernal sadists?

Sometimes I wonder, dear readers, if it might be possible for you to ease your demands on me.

It's as if a plastic bag is around my face, and you are behind me, slowly twisting the handles in your grip until no air can get through.

Let me just say that the ruse worked better than I could have ever hoped.

Isn't that enough to satisfy your morbidity?

Do you require that I detail the squalling tires, the flash of brake lights, the horrible metallic crunch that chased us through the underbrush, horrified at our power?

I didn't know then what would happen.

How could I have known?

I wanted . . . well, I'm not sure what I wanted, but it's over now. I am an adult.

No matter.

It's in the past.

Why do I bring it up?

Because I know that a similar crisis doubtlessly occurred on a certain night for Rico.

The secret night.

Yes!

I will get to it soon enough, but we must, I realize, before then, talk about the other fish in the sea, namely Vita, that crafty minx!

We must also watch out for her in her comment-stream manifestations even to this day!

CHAPTER 14

(SAXAPHONE)

(HIGH HAT)

(MORE SAXAPHONE)

Rico—distraught, adrift—thought that perhaps he would go to Peru.

The "real" had suddenly become elusive.

Yes, he spent hours in a ripe gym and a few days a week "waiting tables," time spent in the midst of sweat, saliva, and excrement, but I could see that it had all begun to feel no different from sitting at his desk with a Stone Age "rolodex" in some municipal office.

Clarity of purpose.

He had lost it.

Corn, on the other hand, knew exactly what he wanted.

He now spent all of his time at Rachil's apartment doing unspeakable acts I still can't quite muster the courage to imagine, so the church sat barren and empty most nights, with only Rico sadly tapping on a snare drum, or idly poking at a TV dinner.

It was a sad scene, so it's no surprise that a neighbor, perhaps that rabble-rouser Tater, somehow convinced Rico to have a party, and though he clearly was in no mood for it, one Friday I saw the church gussied up with "Christmas" lights, a keg. I heard some kind of musical travesty warming up inside.

A party.

Outside, "neighborhood" folks milled about with the sniveling undergrads.

At first, I feared my cover would be blown as I made my way up the drive, but I greeted Tater and Nanez (I believe we had become friends), handed off my "spare" bottle of gin, and then stood sentinel at the keg (the "tap man," coveted position!).

I soon spied poor Rico slumped down on a rusted white aluminum bench the size of a small car that had been delivered from God knows where into the yard.

Jagged pieces of perforated metal hung ragged from the seat, and Rico began running his fingers along the edge.

Slowly.

While men in bandannas and overalls waved tea sticks in the air and heckled one another, Rico clenched his teeth in what seemed to be anticipation of his skin catching a stray piece of bench.

I imagined it would be a triangular piece that would catch his skin, pulling the layers one by one until they loosed a stream of blood, but as his fingers came to the bench edge the disturbed metal settled back into the intended form of the seat, for there was no blood, no tearing.

His hand was intact.

Does a broken chair still contain the essential elements of chairness?

Once a person can no longer sit in it or on it, does it become something else?

It would be called a "broken chair," of course, gaining a modifier and thus complications.

Heart.

Broken heart.

Man.

Married man.

Cuckolded man.

Bereft sad sack.

Is torn skin still skin?

Rico settled back onto the bench, quite upright but not apparently uncomfortably so, and crossed his right leg over his left (what I like to call the French fashion).

His foot bounced along to the rhythm of the band tuning up inside.

In front of him on the gravel drive: a sunburned man with a sunburned child on his shoulders bobbed in time to the beat pouring out from the church.

Where did this man and his child come from?

Who brings a child to a keg party?

This neighborhood continued to baffle me.

"Do you like dancing, buddy?" the man said, eyes turned up to the child.

The child, arms sunk by his sides, on the man's shoulders but with no sense of elation, said nothing.

"Do you like dancing, buddy?" the dad asked again, bobbing faster.

"Everybody dances," the child related glumly, shooting a petulant look, a monumental frown, at Rico, who—finally!—smiled.

The myth of childhood.

Rico surely had begun to know its folly.

This sad little not-dancing child confirmed it.

Wordsworth was an idiot.

Rico took out a cigarette and rolled it between his fingers.

The sun had come down completely, and the cicadas had just begun to pulse.

The mosquitoes.

Maybe, Rico seemed to be thinking, he should just let life take him.

Give in and let whatever would come to him come.

During an argument over which resident had dish duty one night at the church, Corn had patronizingly told Rico that he had no talent for idleness.

"Not a flaw!" Rico had said (true).

Since he was little, Rico said, he woke up every morning with the word "Go" rising steadily out of his consciousness until at last he opened his eyes with it at full volume: "GO!"

But it seemed he had now begun to ask, "Go where?" He could not quite formulate the proper answer, and so here he sat on an aluminum bench trying to mutilate his hands.

Perhaps it was time.

I started to make my way over to him, taking a nip of gin for courage.

His foot jogged at the end of his crossed legs, his fingers tapped at the back of the bench, and anyone watching closely would see that he was licking his lips—one pass over the top with his tongue, then bottom lip over the top, top over the bottom—every few seconds.

The crisis was happening.

But then a voice: "Ugh, it's unpleasant out here. Are you getting eaten alive? Move over."

It was not time!

A slightly plump young woman, a beer in her hand, plopped down on the bench next to Rico, swept her hair up from her neck, and set the floppy mass on top of her head with a sigh.

I paused, swerved back behind the keg, hid.

I took up the tap again but kept an eye on Rico and this plump one, Vita.

I appeared to be at my post only to administer the beer to the growing throng of undergrads trickling in through the weeds, but I was, in fact, taking note.

I saw Rico's eyes flick down and spot the armpit stubble and white clumps of deodorant just above the edge of this woman's bra.

Women were always threatening to burst their self-imposed bonds with hair and sweat and blood!

The potential energy surely thrilled him, just as it did me.

“Why am I even at this lame thing?” she said.

She tilted her head back and stuck a fat tongue out of the side of her mouth, then wrinkled her nose in an attempt to right her listing cat’s-eye glasses.

“Oh right,” she sighed, “I have *a job*.”

She held a Super 8 camera with her left hand and waggled it in the air.

What could she have meant?

Was she documenting the party for the noticeably absent Corn?

Was she employed by some university department to create “fun” montages with wretched soundtracks?

Was she an agent of some kind?

“Why did I agree to do this again?” she sighed, offering no insight as to *whom* she had the agreement with.

Maddening.

Air and foam coughed from the tap.

Rico patted her elbow and offered her a cigarette.

“Because you’re my friend?” he said.

Why?

She looked at the cigarette and let her hair fall around her shoulders.

"Trying to quit, finally, so no. Thank you. I really want to get healthy again. I mean, I'm twenty-two, single, and jobless. I can at least not be a stinky cliché. Whatever. Give it."

He lit it for her.

"So I'm asking all these morons why they're here at this stupid thing, and they're all like 'For the partaaaaaay!' So dumb."

Rico became lost in thought.

"Remember when it seemed so radical to wear a T-shirt with an iron-on?" he asked.

"No."

"Yes you do. I remember you had a shirt that said, 'Mr. Bubble.'"

"That was, like, a reaction against the whole thing, duh."

"I know, but that means, right, that you remember it."

"What's your point?"

"I want to make a T-shirt that really sums up my entire life philosophy. I want a T-shirt that matters."

He looked very serious.

The plump one frowned.

He had to know that she considered him to be smarter than her, and he had to relish this.

She was trying hard to think.

"Wouldn't that just be white? Like, blank?"

"No," he said, "I want words on it. I think that in the future there will be lots of T-shirts with words on them."

"Words or could it just be one word?"

"I think I'd prefer a sentence. In the tradition of the slogan."

They both sat quietly in the evening air as the party began to flood over around them.

I swatted away the cups demanding more beer—couldn't they see I was busy?

"Squirts?" she said, finally.

"With the question mark or no?"

"No, just 'squirts.'"

He laughed.

I laughed.

I poured beer for everyone.

Life made sense again!

Clarity had returned!

Rico would not worry about Rachil, I thought then, he would squirt! We would all squirt! T-shirts would have words on them!

"I think you got it!" he said.

"All right," she said, unaware of her triumph. "I have to go film some more of these jack***es."

She launched herself from the bench and pulled her shirt away from her sweaty back before starting off.

I sprayed beer in her direction, laughing to myself, as a young couple with their plastic cups frowned at me.

"Hey," the plump one yelled out to the couple. "Wanna be famous?"

My elation momentarily thwarted, I ducked out of the way of the camera—what *was* this job she had? Why was I being filmed?

She escorted the couple away from me and began some kind of interview.

Crouched there behind the keg, I pondered her employment.

People who do not like to give their time and energy to a job think of themselves as precious but also damaged, don't you think?

If you value yourself sufficiently, then you know you won't waste time, and so there is no fear of a nine-to-five job.

Now, for example, I love my current task, in part, I know, because I want to love my current task.

I do not want to be a person unhappy in his work, and so I am not.

A strong mind makes for simple choices.

Simple, but not plain.

My job is *just,* and so I am proud of the work I have done—and continue to do—on the blogs.

This woman would clearly never be happy in her work because she didn't (and doesn't still, surely) value herself.

Applying the full force of her mind to a task scares her, and so she always dodges.

Failure is, of course, scary, but so is success.

Any rudimentary analyst could tell you that.

With success comes responsibility, which weak people with no self-worth can't handle, so they invent problems.

People like this plump one, Vita.

And, it must be said, Rico and Nico.

Corn and Chris, if we can compare them in this instance with N/Rico, believe they know who they are.

They have spent sufficient time with their parents, grandparents, and far-off relations, and they have been observant enough to see what each got from whom.

For Corn: his father's peaked upper lip, his grandmother's curly dark hair, his grandfather's smirk, his mother's duplicity.

There is no mystery.

For Rico, two years younger than Corn and of such a dreamy disposition, it was different.

He has never sufficiently known his father, who has had only intermittent contact since the divorce, and this father was replaced, further research has revealed, by a truly bizarre stepfather.

Rico's self has been infused with a cosmic void, unknowable, and thus doubt and weird shame have filled him ever since he was five years old.

Any false start, or hitch in progress, and Rico crumpled.

This is his tragedy, and perhaps why Corn was able to unstring his mind so easily.

Rico looked over at Vita, now slumped in the grass, her shoulders rounded and the hump of her back just before her neck jutted out like a sad bottom lip.

Her parents had clearly retarded her development too.

The couple she had tried to film was fast-walking away, looking scornfully over their shoulders at her, frowning there in the grass.

"Talk to your mother lately?" Rico asked, settling on the grass beside her.

"You don't want to know," she said, slumping further.

True, he didn't (who would?), but that the cliché retort from her was, in fact, the truth made him burst out laughing.

He was, I suspected, becoming the new Rico.

She smiled weakly at him.

He had a loud laugh, a burst of three tiered "ha"s, celebratory and, at the same time, a bit derisive.

He unleashed it only when he seemed truly confident and free.

"Rico," she said, leaning in to put her damp arm around his neck, "I love your laugh! I missed it so much when you were . . ."

She stopped.

No one spoke directly of his time in the hospital.

Instead, she kissed him lightly on the cheek and then pulled back, though not quite fully.

She opened her eyes wide and sucked her cheeks in.

Rico and I both tried not to laugh. I surmised that this must be the plump one's "serious face."

She obviously didn't realize everyone could see how she sucked her cheeks in on purpose, that she looked like some sort of absurd German fashion fish, not, as she must have hoped, like an empathetic compatriot.

"I love you," she said. "For real."

She pouted out her lips.

I guffawed loudly.

"I just want to make sure you know that. I mean, *really* know that . . ."

"I do," he said and pulled her close for another hug.

Over her shoulder, to no one, he had to exercise massive restraint to keep from rolling his eyes.

I rolled mine in solidarity with him.

Love is a force that gives us meaning, isn't that it, dear readers?

No.

That isn't quite right.

Love is a feeling that gives us a fantasy of meaning?

No.

That isn't it either.

Love is an excuse made up by people with meaningless vocations?

Yes.

Rico was now on the precipice of realizing how he could be *above* love.

He would surely have liked to be *in love,* to solve that equation in his life, but he realized now that he could never apply himself to love if it weren't with Rachil.

If he had to follow some kind of love other than Rachil, he would (like me!) love work.

So he would follow work and let love do what it would.

He would follow his instincts and quench his physical desires free of love.

"Oooh," the plump one said, "stupid sunshine."

She touched her hand lightly to her sunburned chest, pulling away from Rico.

"Still hurts?" he asked.

"Mmm hmm."

Why was she sunburned?

We can once again only surmise.

Most likely she had, three days before, drifted down a creek on an intertube with a bottle of Thunderbird and a man she had met the night before. (She looked to be a bit of a slut, so this is extremely plausible.)

She must have fallen asleep halfway through the creek ride, and somewhere along the rest of the way her "boyfriend" had docked his tube and absconded, leaving her to drift in the blazing sun.

I could see the darkish skin beginning to bubble on her neck.

More than three peeling burns in a lifetime and the chances of skin cancer rise exponentially.

My own skin sags and bulges in strange places, but I'm not concerned.

The physical life has little cause for attachment, and so I remain unattached.

For Rico, I'd imagine this unattachment was making him feel like small Mario in the original insipid game he surely loved in high school, blinking out of the visible world, soon to drop off the moving screen.

He hoped that this was in fact the true metaphor, and that this physical life was an avatar for another, further-dimensioned being who was only now connected to "him" via a controller, and once the "Rico" Rico knew flickered and faded, the other being would turn away from the screen, stretch, and go out into the wider world.

"Skin's peeling," he said to Vita.

"So gross. I know."

"Wanna come back to my room and I'll peel it?"

She laughed but then made the earnest fish face, eyes drinking him in.

It was a brute play, ugly, but perhaps it would serve its function and allow Rico to hear the plump one's sex squeals.

"For real," he said and straightened up.

She giggled.

"Sure," she said with a shrug that was anything but casual.

He didn't offer a hand, or say anything further, simply strode across the driveway toward the door.

I sighed, threw down the tap.

Would this job ever end?

It took me nearly fifteen minutes to crawl around back to the "No Trustpassing" side of the church, away from the party, to observe the goings-on in Rico's room, but I made it.

Thankless.

I saw her with a hoop earring dangling from her finger as she plopped backwards onto the thin bedspread.

Rico surely here thought of Corn.

And Rachil.

Theirs was not love but a kind of fatal boredom.

Corn trying to have what he never could when it mattered so much to him, and Rachil letting some combination of pity and lust overtake her reason.

"C'mon, babe," Vita said in a comical sultry hush.

She had pulled her dress off over her head and now lay with her plump legs casually spread, toes wiggling off the side of the bed, bulging panties pushed up toward the ceiling.

He flipped her over.

I admit I was excited for what would happen next.

I saw her buttocks clench and release in anticipation.

Mine did the same.

But, well, I clearly did not understand these two.

Rather than ravish her from behind as any red-blooded male would have done, Rico did only what he said he would do: He straddled her barely covered rump and peeled the burnt skin from her naked back.

That's all!

And as he picked the small sheets of skin from her back, tiny ruffled reverse waves going from breaker to ocean, he told her to close her eyes.

"A tiny dinosaur is harvesting your skin with his tiny toothless beak," he said, "flipping each piece of skin in the air before snapping it up and swallowing it down."

She laughed, said, "Do it, dinosaur, do it!"

He did.

Strange.

CHAPTER 15

I admit things got weird for Rico and me at this time.

What I thought would happen—that he would embark on promiscuous romps with various women and that I would watch—did not happen.

Evidence of these romps, I believed, would cause Rachil to come back to him in a frenzy of jealousy, and so I waited and waited, notebook and recorder in hand.

But I soon came to realize I would perhaps have to adjust my plans, force the issue, take up the cudgel myself, for Rico seemed to merely want to be "friends" with these various young women he knew and spent time with.

One night, as the sun had begun to set on another sexless summer day, Rico had wandered out to the gravel parking lot behind the "Parkside Loco," his shift finally over.

He loafed against a Camaro, slouching in a way I found distasteful—how would he ever win Rachil back with such posture!—but before I could say anything from my spot in the darkness, a young man with slick hair and a put-on sneer walked up, tossing his keys in the air.

"Lookin' for a ride," this greased monkey said to Rico, "or a fight?"

Rico looked him up and down.

"I'm looking for a ride to a fight," he said—witty, to my astonishment—and the boy smiled a queer (yes!) smile as he approached the Camaro.

(Time passed).

(Blood).

I imagined Rico tasted metal at the back of his throat, just as I did there at the "nightclub."

The salt in the sweat on the bristles of his lip—he licked it, swallowed, threw his head so a curly forelock flew back, only to flop forward again.

He smiled and snorted, bounced on the balls of his feet and threw his arms wide.

Dancing to a song with a melodramatic vibrato that pulsed between his legs as I felt it between mine.

I admit, it felt good.

There was little light.

An arm snaked around his waist and disappeared somewhere behind him.

A hot mouth on his earlobe, but later.

Men?

Men!

Of course!

He liked men!

I still hoped he thought of soft girl skin when he kissed these men, when their spiny man-necks were under his fingers, their ****s demanding attention at his belt.

Surely he preferred pliant, crumpling females, but . . . men have something to give and something else to take, true.

I couldn't blame him for wondering.

I wondered myself for a time in my high school years, slyly fondling sleepover mates after they had fallen asleep, comparing our genitalia by heft and caress.

Rico would try to figure it out here, also without light but with cognizant bulging limbs and constant muscles, sweaty pushing in.

In.

In!

Surely, dear readers, you know what it's like?

He would try to decide what kind of power he wanted to give off, what kind to take in.

He would understand the vulnerable when stall-secure, hands on the cool concrete, where an improbably big thing (my word!) would push its way inside him.

To understand the world, one must know both sides of penetration.

This is true.

He was not a violent man.

He did not love.

He secured pleasure.

He intercepted power.

I understood.

I was familiar with this bar, with its ways.

I drank my drink and waited.

Later, breathless, Rico stumbled back toward the church in the dark heat, and I felt the hard bones and muscle lifting off my own body as he surely must have felt too.

It's clear that since adolescence he has had to pluck his eyebrows where they met in the center of his face.

He would have had to grasp each brow hair with tweezers and gently pull.

The sound of the hair sliding in the pore, then the follicle pop.

It left a lovely red welt.

Tweezing was a morning ritual, after shower, before shaving, before dressing for school or work.

The sting was exquisite.

But this summer he stopped.

Just to see, I can imagine, just as he wanted to "see" with men.

Within a month we saw a face that had long threatened to emerge from the morning mirror.

The unibrow.

Crisis.

An odd smudge across his face that caused people to peer into his mien then pull back, startled.

But it had kept the sweat from his eyes at the bar, and in the dark heat of his walk home he rubbed it with gratitude while my own eyes stung (for I pluck and pluck still to this day!).

His body took care to keep his self from experiencing pain.

But the self did not shield his body from pain.

Strange!

The self worried sores and wished, as it did now, for his physical head to split open like a melon and the demon to rise out of the orbital nougat and spend ammunition on the whole stupid town.

Was he gay?

No.

He stuck his arms out straight, fingers flexed, and let out a burred howl, throat burning and buzzing from the night's cigarettes.

A few lights came on in the dark houses, but, despite my own fear of discovery, Rico took no notice.

Grinning, he pulled his fuzzy face into his hands and kept walking blindly down the sleepy streets.

Surely now his mind plunged toward failure, negative thoughts clinging to one another, gathering mass and hurtling toward some disastrous center.

Who was he?

He shook his head and tried to stop his mind with grunts.

I had noticed this happening occasionally, a shame spiral, and when it did happen, when the shame spirals fully sucked him in, he wouldn't emerge from the church for days, no matter the phone calls, the classes, or the job schedules, the hectoring from the window.

We know how it is, don't we, dear readers?

He felt his cells shrivel to tiny currants and blood would wash over everything he saw.

As a child, we would also throw incredible tantrums, holding our breath until we passed out, stomping our army men and kicking anyone hoping to restrain us, would we not?

And, of course, bellowing at the top of our lungs, ragged rage coming through in bleats and sobs.

The tantrums wouldn't erupt when we simply did not get our way; no, they would erupt when we reached the limit of our ability and could go no further.

In my child mind, for example, I could draw Mother's boyfriend with crayon in a perfect likeness—I could see it clearly, the shading on the nose, the eyelashes, the handsome canine-tooth smile beneath the mustache.

It would be perfect.

But then I would begin and each line would be too thick, the sticky crayon smudging the precise marking and then, at last, it would just be a kid's drawing of a man.

Silly.

And little me would erupt wildly when told as much!

Mother would cast my potential stepfather a chilly look and then say to me, "Honey, I'm not going to let you play with the crayons if you're going to get so upset."

A cascade of blocks flung.

A door slammed.

Fat shoes kicked against the wall.

Surely Rico didn't like being this way either, and the shame was what would often keep him in his room.

But the deepest secret of this secret night is not that Rico had been experimenting with the same sex (for we are not so ignorant to the reality of the world as to condemn such experimentation), but that this night of deepest and strangest experimentation is also the night when I took it upon myself to take a more direct role in the proceedings.

I stepped out from the shadows.

“Rico,” I said, “you must get that eyebrow under control.”

For a large boy, he moved surprisingly quickly into a kind of feral crouch, eyes wide and darting.

“Don’t worry,” I said. “I’m a friend. I want to help.”

I offered him a piece of Clark Bar I had been keeping in my pocket.

He pondered it.

“Listen,” I said. “I need to tell you about Rachil.”

His crouch uncoiled, but he remained silent.

The street was a moonscape, asphalt and seedpods.

“Follow me,” I said, and, after a light hesitation, he did.

I clapped him on the shoulder (so tense!) and we made our way slowly back to the church, through the early-morning heat.

Along side streets, while I explained, as delicately as I could, that his best friend was raping his ex-girlfriend repeatedly, he slowly grew comfortable in my presence.

It was like we were old friends!

Of course, I couldn’t offer proof, per se, of the acts I was revealing to him, and I realize now having some documentation would have made my job a bit easier (we seemed to walk for hours), but I eventually convinced Rico through careful and thorough descriptions of the acts I had observed (I admit some embellishments, but the end justified the means).

The poor fool was a blubbering mess by the time we reached his block.

It took even more convincing on my part to keep him from going to the authorities (he had such blind faith in the authorities! Why?), but I eventually pumped him up, got him on his feet, and practically frog-marched him the rest of the way to the church.

We emerged from my well-worn secret path through the neighbor's backyard, and there was Tater, lounging in his army jacket, smoking a tea stick.

He waved to me (not Rico).

Yes, yes, I nodded, waving him off.

The leaves and branches cleared, and we saw through the lighted kitchen window Rachil, on her feet, gesturing wildly with a cigarette in hand, and Corn, seated at the small "dining" table, doubled over in laughter.

Rico paused.

He looked at me with those sad eyes as if to say, "Could it really be true? Look how happy they seem!"

I whispered another choice detail or two from my observations and lo, I'm surprised the privet and scrub didn't swirl into a cyclone behind him, he moved so fast!

I scurried with delight in his wake.

The nervous system!

"I know what you did that night," Rico said, trembling with rage, hulking in the doorway.

Corn and Rachil returned his gaze with ashen faces that went comically agog when I peered over his shoulder.

"Who the **** is that?" Corn said, pointing a twiggy finger.

"I know you," Rachil said, in a kind of shock, "You're . . ."

I smiled as I made my entrance.

"You're that guy from the movie theater!"

I admit that stung a bit.

Yes.

That is all I was to her.

You see, dear readers, it was not yet time for me to reveal my real identity, though, true, I had considered it on the walk over, but it became clear in my mind that I should wait.

She was not ready.

And it's true, I didn't have any reason to believe she would ever be ready, so my plan was to ingratiate myself with her this way and reveal the truth to her some bright afternoon as we walked along the campus, the north side, where the lilacs bloom.

Here at the church, I merely smiled my Matthew Broderick smile.

"At your service," I said and gave a little bow.

As I rose, I saw Rico's right foot upending the table as he lunged for Corn, sending cigarette butts and a (curious) glass of milk to crash and splatter against the wood paneling.

Rico, grown much larger than his effete friend, easily pinned his opponent under his ample belly on the carpet in front of the "stage."

Rico's fighting technique amused me.

I sidled up to Rachil and gave her a dig in the ribs with my elbow and a couple of eyebrow jumps, but she shrank from me, continuing to shriek.

I was a bit put out.

We watched Rico push Corn's face into the carpet, mashing the nose until blood poured forth.

This I liked.

But then, while I yelled "Rapiste!" and clapped my hands together, Rico rotated himself on top of Corn and ripped open the crotch of Corn's khaki shorts with both hands.

Rachil's shrieking achieved a remarkable pitch.

Corn kept up an incessant, breathy mutter: "Get the **** off me; get the **** off me; get the **** off me."

Rico pulled Corn's business out of the hole he had torn in the shorts, reared back, and gave Corn's genitalia one (quite accurate!) punch.

It sounded like a stone dropped into a bowl of pudding from a great height.

I could hardly contain my delight and began emitting my noises, but when I turned to Rachil with a smile, I saw that she was sobbing uncontrollably.

I then aimed my smile at Rico, but he was also in tears, as he reared back once again and thrust his fist forward into Corn's face, which, upon impact, snapped back at an odd angle, then fell with a wet smack against the edge of the stage.

I couldn't have cared less about Corn, but I saw that Rico now turned toward me with rage in his eyes.

The realization crept upon me that I had once again been misunderstood.

I had overestimated humanity.

I had been let down.

Amidst their wailing for me to "Call an ambulance!" I found myself possessed by a force seemingly outside of myself.

A curious glossolalia overcame me as I grabbed Rachil by the arm and spun her toward me (to touch her was divine!).

I gazed into her clear green eyes but felt that some other presence was behind me, gazing through my own (also green!) eyes into hers.

A voice spoke within me.

Was it mine?

No.

I opened my mouth to speak, to let this voice out, but I felt suddenly ill.

I could taste the bottom of my stomach (a cold, milky secretion puddled there), and every pore began filling with heat as a vile flapping belch escaped me, washing over Rachil's closely held face.

She slumped to the floor in a convulsion, and a stabbing pain doubled me over.

I made it only a few steps into the yard before I (shamefacedly) wretched.

Through the spittle and bile I yelled to the imbeciles, "Don't look at me!" to no avail.

There are times when vomiting is the end of a journey, when it signals the end of a long episode of internal roiling; afterwards, relief engulfs one's body like a cool bath on a sweltering day.

This was not one of those times.

This upheaval signaled, rather, a journey's beginning, the first step on the rest of my life's path.

I stumbled into the street and vomited once more, this time a curiously red mixture, tangy and sour, with tickly lumps.

I tried to catch the expulsion in my hands, but the gesture proved futile and most of the vomit splashed onto my right leg, hot at first, but quickly cool, a tepid caking.

I looked back at my confreres, but it was as if I were trying to read a street sign from behind an aquarium (I've thought long and hard about what exactly this blurring resembled, and I believe this aquarium analogy is remarkably astute), yet despite it all I could still just make out two watery figures standing in the doorway of the church, silhouetted once again by the kitchen light.

I reached out my hand, knowing I wouldn't of course be able to touch them but wanting some acknowledgment that they were and would be watching over me should unconsciousness overtake me, as seemed imminent.

I saw the dull blade of Rico's outline lean into sloping Rachil's before ushering her back inside to, no doubt, care for the bleeding Corn.

I attempted to speak but out came a flood of other matter.

I collapsed.

From the warm, now-wet concrete I could see the door to the church shutting me out forever.

There was a profound sadness all around, dripping from the trees.

I could hear it, and the sound was nearly death itself.

I again tried to catch the matter pouring from my mouth but I found my hands had gone numb.

I sprang up with the last of my energy and ran for what felt like hours but was surely only a few blocks until the numbness spread to my legs, then my face.

All was a fuzzed blank, but it proved only a temporary respite from the pain, for within seconds my muscles began to seize within my skin—every bit of meat, from my quadriceps to my dorsals, became rigid, my face became a rictus of pain, and I found I could no longer open my eyes.

I felt more matter violently leaving my face by way of my flared nostrils, but I couldn't move my hands to stop the expulsion.

It's a curious sensation to finally understand how you will die.

Not the manner in which you will die—which becomes suddenly irrelevant, FYI—but rather how you will feel and what you will think at the instant when life ceases, whenever that time might occur.

In this case, while my external circumstances were quite dramatic—as I assume they will be when the true moment of my death arrives—internally, I was taking a rather calm accounting of my situation; I was able to assess my physical status and conclude that the whole episode was inane.

The fuzzing and blurring of my vision, the rigid calcifying of my musculature, the sudden inside-out nature of my digestion—it was all just stupid.

This is the height of idiocy, I thought. A muddled and inappropriate procedure.

Now, looking back, I understand that this is how it feels to die, how Corn surely must have felt there in the church, bleeding on the stage.

In an idiotic fit of dimness and confusion, while one's attention is elsewhere, life will leave through an unseen exit.

You too, dear readers, will die this way.

The body fails and the mind registers its disappointment, its disapproval, and then . . . well, that is the more interesting question, isn't it?

What happens after the dull slip of life from one's body?

Do you believe in an afterlife, dear readers?

In heaven?

In hell?

You might stop to consider the possibilities.

I believe in a long gray corridor where time does not exist.

Whether this is heaven or hell I do not know, nor did I, at this moment, when the disorder reached its moronic climax, get a chance to find out, for I was spared.

I soon heard sirens, tires squealing, the crunch of boots on concrete, and then I was jostled.

Gruff voices asked me obvious questions ("Are you okay?" "Can you hear me?" "Can you move your arms?").

My facial muscles remained locked, so I merely tried to exhale loudly from my nose to signal my exasperation (and that I was, in fact, alive).

More matter squished from me instead, and I noted the gruff voices register disapproval at the mess I had apparently made.

I made a mental note to let the departments responsible know that I didn't appreciate their minions' haughtiness and inattention at that moment (fear not, I let them know!).

I also did not appreciate the minions' response to the next moment when further matter exited my person through my stinging and tender rear end.

Loaded into the ambulance, IVs were administered and further questions asked.

I must have lost consciousness at some point, because the next moment I remember, my eyes did finally open to reveal watery shapes, blobs of color floating above me like fleshy balloons.

Feeling had returned to my limbs, but just barely, so I found that despite all my efforts, my arms would only strike out spasmodically at seemingly random intervals, my legs jerk up to my chest, etc. I tried to speak but could only cry out in gasping rhythms.

What did I want to say?

I am only somewhat ashamed to admit that I wanted to say I had once again soiled myself and at that moment I felt the soilage seeping to unsavory places, stinging in my crevices. The thinner blog (Dear me! Blog! I meant to type "blob"! Paging Dr. Freud!!!) above me murmured at my screams while the fatter one cooed, but neither solved the equation.

My hand.

I could point, couldn't I? I tried but nothing of note occurred. Perhaps this was simply my lot, to lie in filth. I began to sob quietly to myself, warm tears in rivulets down my temples.

There's an odd comfort to crying, a loosening of the strictures around one's heart; I've never been ashamed of it, and in this case I felt it calming me.

Someone would eventually clean me; I was in a hospital after all, and that is what members of the hospital staff do (though suddenly I couldn't detect any hospital staff about).

The lights had dimmed but for the soft glow of the TV my "roommate" (heretofore undetected) had on.

I felt a sigh escape me, and my head began to sit heavily on my neck. My legs began to relax, and a calm lightness suffused my person. Sleep would soon come.

Peace.

No, alas—my arm swung up in a massive twitch, sending my hand directly into my (apparently) open mouth. The meat just below my thumb and forefinger landed flush between my teeth, and I bit down furiously.

The pain was a cartoon police siren, all red and wailing, the sharp pierce of skin, the dull crunch and pop of the gristly corpuscles as I chomped and chomped, muffling my cries with hand-flesh.

The lights came up in a rush and the blobs came back loud and direct.

My entire face felt wet when they pulled my hand away, and I felt my legs kick out, my back arch rigid.

The pain was exquisite, so I shut my eyes tight and tried to concentrate on its intricacies, to detail them in my cries.

No one understood . . .

Enough.

ENOUGH!

Stop pulling at me, readers, stop tugging with your phantom fingers my very bones.

I won't let you jerk them out of my body to suck the marrow dry!

Do you think I can't feel it?

You can't have me!

Some things remain private.

What else do you want me to divulge?

Don't you have enough by this point to satisfy your wretched needs?

Stop reading, why don't you?

Go away!

Leave me alone!

Ah, but why worry?

You don't know a thing.

Read on if you must.

Take it!

It's nothing.

The real me escapes every time.

I can't stop your pursuit, I know.

You will continue to press yourselves into me in a vain attempt to understand this real me, but you will only find wisps of smoke and embers at the end of your journey, just like my mother.

Thirty years ago, she read the "hurtful" things I had written about her in my private journal, and our relationship was ruined forever after.

What did I write?

Was it my fault, after all?

Wouldn't you like to know, hateful reader, but I'll never tell, for some things, I've learned, must remain private, for their revelation destroys, such as was the case when I put too much trust in my mother's virtue.

I had such a journal then—leather bound with a black binding, gold-embossed lettering on the front declaring it to be "My Personal Journal" in cursive lettering—and I filled it with every transmission, every thought, every argument that caromed down the colonnades of my mind.

Some days I would simply look back over the pages and marvel at my erudition and wit, just as you surely do here, but then one morning—a wet Saturday in drab November—I absentmindedly left this journal on the shabby afghan atop my twin bed in my room while I went out for my weekly trip to the record store to—I remember it so well!—see what new arrivals the doughy clerk had chucked in the bins.

When I returned, I knew what hell was.

For years afterwards, dread and paranoia lurked behind my writing hand, for any word or combination of words might be exposed, misunderstood once again, inviting my mother's wrath, streaking sobs and pleading, tearing fingernails and lipsticked teeth upon me like a briney fisherman's net, suffocating me ever more despite my thrashing.

In fact, my behavior toward Corn and Rachil can be partially explained by this dread, if one cared to explain it.

My mother said I had "ruined everything" and that she was "horrified" by what I had written, though surely no adolescent boy had NOT had similar thoughts, though I do know now that not every adolescent boy has the mind or courage to explore them.

Think of the safety I must have felt that I COULD explore such thoughts!

Isn't that worth anything?

Well, that safety was exploded by prying eyes.

Once my words had been wrenched from their private world, I no longer felt in control of the narrative of my life, and for someone who had long considered himself a master of narrative, this was a crushing blow; I spent the rest of my time in that house shuffling along in a stupor, the two of us, my mother and I, avoiding each other at all costs until the day I moved out with only a JanSport backpack, a Walkman, and a sense of integrity to my name.

My "story" by that time had become not the one I told myself privately, but rather some misbegotten version dimly perceived by an overemotional harpy.

I felt for years I was doomed to be misunderstood, and, the worst tragedy was further writing and "expression" only seemed to make it worse.

Since all I had ever done was write in an attempt to give shape to what felt like the lurching chaos of my time, without writing I was only an empty shell of myself, pasted down by depression and lethargy.

All because of my "journal"!

*

Dear readers, I've recessed—no, that is not the right word—recused?—yes—recused—I have recused myself from continuing this comment.

I have become too caught up in the frenzy, and I find myself trying to impress you (why?) and therefore lying to you, saying things at a frenzied clip that are not true, which make me sound as base and vile as the creature I have sworn myself against.

This fact, which I admit only came upon me gradually, like some kind of neuralgia, has shaken me to my core.

Every act, understand, from the click of a keystroke to the slinging of a Molotov cocktail, has importance.

Let's not forget the sparrow.

I believe in the sparrow.

There is judgment.

I'm not so childish as to believe in an old man God with a white beard and robe like a movie Zeus in sandals watching the actions of the world with a dispassionate eye, but there is a judging presence.

I believe in justice.

And while I am sure that time will ultimately take care of the unjust, I am sensitive.

When injustice appears in my world, it affects me.

It is uncomfortable, to say the least.

My back aches, my scalp itches.

I develop ulcers in my mouth, gas pains in my abdominal region.

My jaw clenches for hours.

I get painful daylong erections and headaches.

I would gladly suffer if I felt that simple suffering were the purpose, but once I speak out, once I do in fact act against injustices—all in a flash my symptoms disappear.

It's as if my entire being goes slack like a rag doll and a startling peace overtakes me.

It's as if I have just awoken in a dewy field with the summer sun on my naked body.

This is the presence of the divine judge acknowledging my work.

I'm sure of it.

The divine is acknowledging me, my existence, and it is forgiving me my past injustices.

But only because I am now on the righteous path.

It may come as a surprise, but these feelings—the overwhelming discomfort and torpor—I did not always know the proper way to relieve them.

I am ashamed.

I am guilty.

There's nothing you can say or do to make me feel any less shame or guilt, which is why it makes so little sense for me to have lied to you.

I can't expect you to understand, but your immediate understanding has never been my goal.

There is more to the story.

Those boys.

They were not quite as I've described them, it's true, but I wasn't completely dishonest about them, either.

I may have misrepresented things.

But how ominous I sound!

That's all so far in the past, I don't even know why I'm prattling on and on about it, burrowing into that pulsing, crazed tunnel of memory—and for what?

So that I might confess to you my sins?

As if you deserve it?

One should confess to a priest or a shaman, not some silly pack of girls on the internet!

Of course I mean no offense, and I hope you embrace both your silliness and your girlishness, for not everyone is so lucky as to be afforded the luxury of either!

I see you there with your coltish charm, looking offended, wishing you could go back to the original blog post as if you had never entered into my comment.

Don't be offended!

I am flattering you!

Take it!

I admit that I wake up some mornings with phrases chattering through my mind.

Passwords perhaps?

I go to the wedding site and I try them out, but so far the transmissions have been imperfect.

What would I do if I were able to infiltrate the enemy?

I've dreamt of simply adding a choice comma to the latest egregious excretion, of copying all the back-end text and redeploying it on my own site, to take it over under another name, but my choicest fantasy is simply to delete, to delete all with a series of joyous keystrokes and clicks—so effortless!—each one like ballast thrown over the bow of my soul.

Just to write it leaves me nearly breathless.

But alas.

The passwords do not work, and it is worse that I have tried.

Afterwards I am brought terribly low by a feeling of futility.

The site rages on and each posting, every comment, is a direct attack on my psyche.

Must I run away to maintain my sanity?

No, of course not.

But what can I do?

Any reaction will only embolden that wretched sack of excrescence, and so I must outwardly be perceived as ignoring him—*oh yes it is nothing ho hum I never even think of it*—and somehow try to stay ahead of the game.

So I publish my own series of sites with just my name printed over and over and over again.

I must admit that I am powerless to do anything else.

The feeling is eerily similar to a kind of overwhelming guilt.

When guilt becomes overwhelming does it turn to shame?

Very well then, shame.

I will admit there are things I am ashamed of, things I have done or in some cases—so much worse, I realize now!—allowed to happen.

How could it be worse to have not done some terrible act than to have done it?

If you have to ask, then I'm afraid you are more pitifully naïve than I first thought.

The site is at zero. I should have seen the signs.

When confronted with this volatile mix of intelligence and creativity, that niggling functionary should have only sat back in awe, but very slowly he realized that his role as facilitator and moderator was not enough for him—he wanted control!

He wanted glory!

He wanted fame and a name for himself and so he stopped dealing with me honestly.

He put my comments "in moderation" for days at a time so a long queue would build up—maddening!—and then he began to delete, systematically erasing me from the conversation.

I should have known that once he was pressed he would revert to type, a deluded usher for the status quo, no better than any of the myriad other site moderators and administrators who have given me a similar ticket.

Doesn't anyone have courage?

Won't anyone else stand up to these fiends?

I ask, but of course I know the answers already.

There is no one.

Not every night, but most, I dream of pursuit.

Sometimes it's a ridiculous stock character from a popular entertainment—the Blob, the Creature from the Black Lagoon, the 50 Foot Woman—but it always moves slowly and methodically in stark contrast to my hysterical huffing and puffing to get away.

The feeling is real, and more often than not I awaken after I have been cornered—finally and fatally—by my pursuer.

It would be naïve to think this pursuit did not continue into my waking life.

I am pursued.

Ever so badly I would like to be found out, to be caught, so whatever the pursuer wishes done to me could be done, and then whatever is next would come, the pursuit finally over.

A cascade of relief falls over me at that simple thought, the imagined falling away of this perpetual fear, like a car encrusted with a layer of ice and snow out on the interstate for an hour until finally—in a flash of white and sparkle—the trapezoidal weight flies free, end over end, plunges down, and finally smashes in a burst on the road just passed, behind, gone for good.

I'm nearly weeping as I write this—no, I admit it, I am weeping—just to think there could be an end to the feeling.

Of course, there is occasional respite but no real end.

I know, even as we head into a new decade, that the pursuit will continue.

It is inside.

And so it is endless.

COLOPHON

The More You Ignore Me was designed at
Coffee House Press, using QuarkXPress 7.5
on an iMac with an Intel Core 2 Duo processor
with a speed of 2.66 GHz.
The text is set in Adobe Caslon.

COMMENTS

TL;DR

THANK YOU TO OUR GENEROUS FUNDERS

Coffee House Press is an independent, nonprofit literary publisher. Our books are made possible through the generous support of grants and gifts from many foundations, corporate giving programs, state and federal support, and through donations from individuals who believe in the transformational power of literature. Coffee House Press receives major operating support from Amazon, the Bush Foundation, the National Endowment for the Arts, the Jerome Foundation, the McKnight Foundation, from Target, and in part from a grant provided by the Minnesota State Arts Board through an appropriation by the Minnesota State Legislature from the State's general fund and its arts and cultural heritage fund with money from the vote of the people of Minnesota on November 4 2008, and a grant from the Wells Fargo Foundation of Minnesota. Coffee House also receives support from: several anonymous donors; Elmer L. and Eleanor J. Andersen Foundation; Around Town Agency; the E. Thomas Binger and Rebecca Rand Fund of the Minneapolis Foundation; the Patrick and Aimee Butler Family Foundation; the Buuck Family Foundation, Dorsey & Whitney, LLP; Fredrikson & Byron, P.A. the Kenneth Koch Literary Estate; the Lenfestey Family Foundation; the Nash Foundation; the Rehael Fund of the Minneapolis Foundation; Schwegman, Lundberg & Woessner, P.A.; the Archie D. & Bertha H. Walker Foundation; the Woessner Freeman Family Foundation; and many generous individual donors.

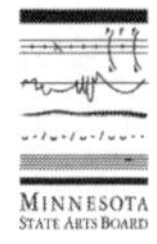

amazon.com

COFFEE HOUSE PRESS PUBLISHERS CIRCLE

The Publishers Circle is an exclusive group recognizing those individuals who make significant contributions to Coffee House Press's annual giving campaign. Understanding that a strong financial base is necessary for the press to meet the challenges and opportunities that arise each year, this group plays a crucial part in the success of our mission.

Suzanne Allen
Patricia and John Beithon
Bill Berkson and Connie Lewallen
E. Thomas Binger and Rebecca Rand
Ruth and Bruce Dayton
Mary Ebert and Paul Stembler
Chris Fischbach and Katie Dublinski
Doug France
Sally French
Glenn Miller and Jocelyn Hale
Nina Hale and Dylan Hicks
Roger Hale and Nor Hall
Randy Harten and Ron Lutz
Anselm Hollo and Jane Dalrymple-Hollo
Jeffrey Hom
Carl and Heidi Horsch
Alex and Ada Katz
Stephen and Isabel Keating
Robert and Margaret Kinney
Kenneth Kahn
Allan and Cinda Kornblum
Seymour Kornblum and Gerry Lauter
Kathy and Dean Koutsky
Jim and Susan Lenfestey
Carol and Aaron Mack
Mary McDermid
Sjur Midness and Briar Andresen

Peter and Jennifer Nelson
Joyce Rude
Sam Savage
John Sjoberg and Jean Hagen
Kiki Smith
Marla Stack and Dave Powell
Jeffrey Sugerman and Sarah Schultz
Patricia Tilton
Marjorie Welish
Stu Wilson and Mel Barker
Warren Woessner and Iris Freeman
Margaret and Angus Wurtele
Betty Jo Zander and Dave Kanatz

To you and our many readers across the country, we send our thanks for your continuing support.

OUR MISSION

Coffee House Press publishes exciting, vital, and enduring authors of our time; we delight and inspire readers; we contribute to the cultural life of our community; and our books enrich our literary heritage. By building on the best traditions of publishing and the book arts, we produce books that celebrate imagination, innovation in the craft of writing, and the many authentic voices of the American experience.

For more information about the Publishers Circle and ways to support Coffee House Press's books, authors, and activities, please visit coffeehousepress.org or contact us at: info@coffeehousepress.org

Join us in our mission at coffeehousepress.org

TRAVIS NICHOLS RECOMMENDS THESE COFFEE HOUSE PRESS BOOKS

The Meat and Spirit Plan, by Selah Saterstrom

"*The Meat and Spirit Plan* is ferocious and dazzling, the work of a savage poet. Every scene is a hard polished gem of raunch and revelation. Strung together they build a force of piercing tenderness. It's an impressive achievement, and a real pleasure to read."

—**Katherine Dunn**, author of *Geek Love*

On the Planet without Visa, by Sotère Torregian

"In Sotère Torregian, we have not simply one of the most unique poets of the New York School, but one of the most unique poets writing today. For I know no other poet who has so melded the quotidian impulse of Frank O'Hara . . . with the full tilt madness of authentic surrealism."

—**The City Lights Booksellers & Publishers Blog**

Drowning Tucson, by Aaron Michael Morales

"*[Drowning Tucson]* presents characters with depth and awareness who refuse to be defined by their circumstances, even when they cannot escape them. Morales, in a style reminiscent of Hubert Selby Jr. *(Last Exit to Brooklyn)*, vividly details a community's beauty and brutality."

—***Chicago Tribune***